A FAMILY AFFAIR

Book Two of The Blue Hat Detective Agency

Meagan Diehl

*To my husband for not letting me quit, and to my
mom and dad for believing in me.
I couldn't have done this without you.*

May 2021

He looked around the room. Everyone was happy to be there. They were reliving their favorite high school moments, and he was constantly being mentioned *in* said memories.

Why couldn't Barbara see how much people loved him?

Why did she have to take Jessie?

"Whoa! I haven't seen you in *forever*, man! How've you been? How's Barbie?" He smiled a fake smile at his old friend.

"She's good. Our sitter canceled at the last minute, so she stayed home. How's everyone there?" He waited, bored out of his mind, as he was told about how things were going perfectly. Businesses were taking off. Families were growing. Everyone was just... happy.

He was the favorite in school- the funny guy, the leader, the star football player.

Why were *they* successful? Why was his life falling apart?

He gave another fake smile at the pictures.

Wait... She looked a little like Jessie. He started paying more attention.

"... Just turned twelve last month! They're our youngest two, but definitely the apples of our eyes. I can't imagine them not being in my life."

But he was never home, or his business wouldn't be doing so well... He didn't deserve two beautiful little girls. None of them deserved their children. Not when Jessie was taken from him like he was incapable of being a father.

CHAPTER 1

"Happy birthday, Jimmy," Nick said again, bending down to hug his son. Jimmy tried wrapping his arms around Nick, but still couldn't seem to make it past his father's muscular shoulders. Jimmy let go and leaned back in his bed, stretching out his brand new catcher's mitt from his grandfather.

"Thanks, Dad."

"I just can't believe you're fourteen. I still remember when your mom told me she was pregnant with you." Jimmy gave his father a small smile. It was the same for every birthday. Not that Jimmy minded. He knew his dad had loved his mom. Had it not been for the drunk driver who killed her when he was three, they would probably still be together, after all.

"Grandpa and I are still ok to go to Kings Dominion tomorrow, right?"

"Yeah. I've got some stuff to do at the office. He said he'd pick you up around eight. Are you sure you're not upset I'm not going?"

"It's fine. You and Grandpa have gotten better, but it's still not smart to have you two together with no way to escape." Nick smirked.

"I suppose that's true. Alright, kid. Get some

sleep, ok?"

"I'll try. Lucy's cake was… I think she used too much sugar." Nick chuckled at his wife's lack of baking abilities.

"Maybe next year, we'll just get a store-bought one like we usually do. Sound ok?"

"*Please*." Shaking his head, Nick bent down and kissed Jimmy's temple.

"Night, Jim. Love you."

"Night. Love you, too. And tell Lucy thanks for trying. It meant a lot to me."

"I will." Nick turned off the light and closed the door behind him.

"The cake was that bad?" Nick turned and saw Lucy standing in the hall, teary eyed.

"No, Luce. It was fine. We're just not used to someone making us cakes. I've never been one for the oven, so since his fourth birthday, it's been made at the store. Now he has a mom to do it again, and it'll take some getting used to. Promise."

"I'm sorry, Nick. Everything has just been so scattered lately and I probably did add too much sugar, and-"

"*Hey*," Nick said, grabbing her hands. "It was great. I'm happy to take a piece to work tomorrow, too."

"Promise?"

"I do." Nick kissed her cheek and smiled at her. "I'm going to go clean up. You should go relax in the bath. I know you bought some new candles, and there's a bottle of wine-" Nick frowned at the emphatic shaking.

"I think I might just go to bed. I'm not feeling well."

"You sure?" Nick felt her forehead. "You feel cool to me."

"Just because I don't have a fever doesn't mean I don't feel well," Lucy snapped.

"I didn't… I just wanted to make sure I didn't need to get my dad here to keep an eye on Jimmy so I could take you to the emergency room. I didn't mean you weren't sick, love." Lucy sighed.

"I'm going to bed."

"I'll be there in a bit." Lucy nodded and walked down the hall. Nick watched her go, concerned at her behavior, before turning and going into their dining room. He scraped the leftover food on the plates into the trash and put the dishes in the dishwasher. Nick looked at the rectangular blue frosted cake on the counter and swallowed thickly. It was by far the worst thing he'd tasted since his mother-in-law gave him food poisoning. Lucy was adamant it was an accident, but Mrs. Montgomery never liked him. Even now, and they'd been together for over four years! But Nick sighed and covered the cake, determined to choke it down for the sake of his wife's feelings. He had just finished wiping down the table when he felt his phone buzz.

"Smith," he answered, assuming it was his father or brother calling at this hour.

"*Nick Smith?*"

"Speaking."

"*My name is Frances Hannen. My daughter is missing, and I was told you could help me.*"

"Locating missing people isn't really my specialty, ma'am. Have you talked to the police?"

"*They keep telling me there's nothing they can do without proof and to assume she's just run away. Please, Mr. Smith. I read where you caught a murderer who had been killing people for thirty years when the FBI couldn't-*"

"Mrs. Hannen, that man had killed my own mother. I had a vested interest in taking him down."

"*But you still got him. Please, Mr. Smith. My daughter is all I have. She's been missing for four days, now.*" Nick tossed down the rag he'd been using to wipe the table and rubbed his forehead with the back of his hand.

"Where are you located, ma'am?"

"*I'm in Louisa County. In Virginia.*"

"My office is located in Leesburg. I'll be in there at eight tomorrow. Can you meet me at some point?"

"*I can do that. Thank you, Mr. Smith.*"

"Don't thank me yet," Nick said, cringing as his father seemed to come out of his mouth. He'd been spending too much time with him. "Please bring a picture of your daughter, any electronics she might have that you're comfortable with me going through, and if possible, a diary."

"*I can do that,*" she repeated. "*I'll be there at*

eight sharp."

"Then I'll see you in the morning." Nick hung up and rolled his shoulders before dialing his father's number.

"Johns."

"It's me. How refundable are those tickets to Kings Dominion?"

"Damn it, Nicky. I can't reschedule on him again."

"You were the one who wanted to be a consultant-"

"Occasionally, and when you needed *me. Do you actually need me tomorrow, or am I some sort of deflection again?"*

"Wow. Most dads who've abandoned their kids for thirty years would be happy said kids want their help. Must be mistaken-"

"Most kids whose dads jump in front of them to save their lives are usually happy to let the past stay in the past," Mason countered. Nick rolled his eyes.

"I've got a woman coming in tomorrow from Louisa saying her daughter's missing. She said cops are saying it's a runaway case. You're former FBI. Isn't this an area of expertise?" Nick could hear Mason sigh.

"I'll look over your notes when we get back, son, but I've already rescheduled Kings Dominion three times now. I'm not doing it again. It won't be long before he's in college, and with Nicky in Florida... He's the only grandkid I get to spoil-"

"I'm your *son-"*

"You're forty, as you often feel the need to remind me. Jimmy's fourteen."

"Ok. Get in after dinner and we'll get a beer, I guess. I'll go over the case with you then- if there *is* a case."

"I can do that. Please make sure Jimmy knows it's his show tomorrow."

"When is it *not*?" Nick asked, rolling his eyes. "I'll see you in the morning, Dad. Night." Nick hung up and sighed. He put the rag in the hamper by the washing machine and stripped to his boxers before trudging to his bedroom. He climbed into bed and put his phone on the charger.

"Who was on the phone?" he heard Lucy ask in her soft voice.

"Some woman asking for help finding her daughter. I know business has been better since the trial, but I feel like I have no peace, now."

"I'm sure Mason will help-"

"He's taking Jim to Kings Dominion. I tried."

"Ok. I'll come in tomorrow and do what I can-"

"It's fine, babe. You had scheduled tomorrow off forever ago. I'm not going to take that back just because people act like I'm famous now. I mean, it was *one* trial. It's ridiculous. At least everyone *here* still acts normal-"

"That's because they expected you to get him," Lucy smiled. "You were already their hero before Anderson came to town." Nick scowled.

"I thought we agreed not to mention his

name in our bed?" Lucy put her head on Nick's chest.

"He can't get to us anymore."

"But this is supposed to be the one place I feel safe, Luce. I can't when I'm thinking of him." Lucy kissed his lips.

"Still thinking about him?"

"Yes." She kissed his jaw.

"Still?"

"Yes." She kissed down his neck, laughing as he changed their positions so she was on her back.

"There you are," she said, eyes twinkling. Nick leaned down and captured her lips in a kiss.

"I'd be happy to continue, but you said you weren't feeling well," he whispered in her ear.

"Maybe tomorrow," she said. Nick kissed her cheek and settled in beside her, wrapping a protective arm around her.

"Night, Lucy. Love you."

"Night, Nick. Love you, too." Nick closed his eyes and willed himself to sleep, completely missing Lucy placing a hand on her lower abdomen and sighing.

CHAPTER 2

"Shit!" Nick cried. He grabbed a napkin from the seat beside him and tried to sop up the coffee he had spilt on his pants. "Great," he groaned. He got out of his car and scowled his way to the door of his office. He could still see the old sign for 'Smith Detective Agency.' He and Mason had decided to rename it the 'Blue Hat Detective Agency,' as Nick and Mason refused to change their names. This fit them better, as they still both wore their Tar Heels hats constantly, though Nick's current hat was newer than the one he used to wear. Nick unlocked his office and walked in, turning the lights on as he went through the rooms.

He went in his office and looked in the small closet, hoping he had a spare pair of pants without coffee stains. Finding none, he sighed as he pulled out his phone, calling his wife.

"Hey. How'd the coffee run go? I'm sorry- I promise I'll get more grounds today-"

"Actually, I was hoping for a new pair of pants. They decided they wanted the coffee more than my mouth." Nick heard the snickering and scowled. "It's not funny, Lucy. I've got a meeting in ten minutes-" A knock interrupted him. "Make that a meeting *now*. Can you have Mason drop off a pair of pants- Scratch that. Can *you* bring me some so I don't feel like my dad is bringing me pants at school?" Full blown laughter met his ear and Nick pulled the phone away, scowling.

"I'll bring you a pair in a few minutes," Lucy finally said. *"I'm sorry, Nick. The way you just described it-"* Nick rolled his eyes at the deep belly laughs.

"Laugh all you want, but *please* don't tell Dad. I haven't lived down the soda exploding on me-"

"Too late. Sorry." The knock came again.

"I've got to go. Can't wait to explain why I smell like coffee and look like I pissed myself."

"I'll be there in a minute, babe." Nick hung up and opened the door.

"Mrs. Hannen?"

"Yes. But please, call me Fran." The middle aged woman with red hair walked into his office.

"Nick," he said, sticking his hand out to her. "I apologize for my state of dress. I had someone in front of me slam on their brakes and coffee went everywhere."

"It happens to everyone. And as long as your investigative skills are better than your coffee drinking skills, we'll be fine." Nick smiled as he felt his face heat up.

"Why don't we go into my office? It's a bit more comfortable in there." Mrs. Hannen nodded and carried the things she'd brought into Nick's office. Nick sat behind his desk and Mrs. Hannen sat across from him, putting a laptop and photo on the desk in front of her.

"She... Her diary is on her computer." Nick nodded.

"Let's start with a name," he said, getting out a pad of paper and a pen. "And any physical characteristics you can think of that aren't easily seen in a photograph."

"Her name is Abby- Abigail Hannen. She's fifteen and about to start her sophomore year in high school. She's in the top of her class and taking her first advanced placement class this year. And she runs track for the school."

"Ok," Nick said, writing the information down. "When did you last see her?"

"She was getting ready to go to a movie with a friend, Ronnie- Veronica, on Sunday afternoon. Ronnie said she never showed up."

"Just so I have a better understanding, is Veronica someone who would lie to cover for your daughter?"

"Absolutely not. At least... not to me, Mr. Smith."

"And are there any boyfriends I should know about?" He asked, looking at the picture of the young girl. She had red hair, just like her mother, and freckles all across her face.

"None that I know of," Mrs. Hannen admitted.

"Fran, are you and your daughter close?"

"We are. Since my husband passed three

years ago, it's just been us. We've had to rely on each other more than anyone..."

"My first wife passed when my son was three," Nick said. "I understand." Mrs. Hannen nodded.

"She's a good girl, Nick. She always texted me when she was leaving, when she got where she was going, if there was any type of delay... And I never had to *ask*! She wouldn't have just *disappeared*!" Mrs. Hannen put her face in her hands and wept. Nick, feeling uncomfortable, handed her a tissue box.

"I'm sure she's fine. But I'll look into this. I have a contact who is a former FBI agent. I'll run this by him-"

"The FBI agent from the case?" Nick gave her a fake smile.

"That's the one."

"Will he actually be able to help?"

"He will. He's taking a personal day today, but I've already set up a meeting to go over this information tonight. I'll look at your daughter's computer and her emails- everything that's available to me here. Tomorrow, I'll visit Louisa and talk with her friends. Would you mind letting them know? And their parents. I'm not a *cop*, and therefore it's not exactly illegal for me to question minors without guardians present, but I prefer to have another adult nearby. It's the same courtesy I would ask for for my fourteen year old."

"I'm sure the other parents would appreciate

that. I'll be sure to let them know. Thank you, Mr. Smith."

"Like I said, don't thank me yet." Nick heard the bell chime over his door and looked up as Lucy walked in with a new pair of pants.

"Good morning, Mr. Smith," she said with a knowing smile.

"Good morning," he grinned back. "Mrs. Hannen, this is my assistant, Lucy. If you call the office, it'll most likely be her that you speak with."

"It's nice to meet you," Lucy said. "Mr. Smith, where would you like your pants?" she asked with a smirk.

"I'll take them," he told her, rolling his eyes. "Go enjoy your day. Let me know if Mason or Jimmy call?"

"I will," she replied, giving him a chaste kiss on his cheek. Lucy nodded to Mrs. Hannen and left the office.

"Your assistant, hm?" Mrs. Hannen said with a wry grin.

"She's also my wife," Nick admitted with a smile. "I'll call you if I have any questions about your daughter. If you think of anything, please don't hesitate to call me or the office."

"Thank you."

"Please-"

"No, Nick. You're the first one to *listen* to me and act on my words instead of waiting for a ransom note. For that, I thank you." Nick shrugged.

"I wasn't listened to by cops, either. Had I been, my mother might have been the only victim of Phil Anderson. Even if there's nothing else I can do, I *can* listen."

"And that's why you came highly recommended."

"May I ask who recommended me?"

"Oh, I looked you up on the internet. Your reviews are amazing. And I know I owe you for this meeting, but the rest-"

"I do ask for a down payment, but for a missing child, I'll be fine to wait for everything after she's returned to you. My... consultant had missing children and hired a private investigator to find them, and the man bled my friend dry with no results. After hearing that, anything involving children, I prefer to wait until I have results. I hope that won't be a problem."

"Of course not. Thank you, Nick. I was worried about scraping enough together-"

"All you need to concern yourself with right now is your daughter. And I promise, when she comes home, the bill won't be as much as you think," Nick said, already considering waiving his fees for the woman. "It was nice meeting you, though I wish it had been under better circumstances. I will keep you updated with what I find." Mrs. Hannen nodded and left the office. Nick waited for her to leave before quickly changing his pants. He threw the coffee soaked ones back in his car so they wouldn't be forgotten in the office and went back to his desk. Nick then opened the laptop and began his initial investigation.

CHAPTER 3

There was nothing of importance on the computer, Nick realized several hours later. He rubbed his burning eyes and closed the laptop. This girl, Abby, was as squeaky clean as they came. Nick was sure even *Jimmy* wasn't as innocent as she was. There were no hidden files. The 'diary' entries discussed crushes, but no secret boyfriend- at least for her. Her friend Veronica apparently had one. Nick had made a note to ask the girl the following day, once again thankful Jimmy was a boy and not as dramatic as these young girls. He started to pack the laptop and his notes to head back to the house to eat lunch with Lucy when there was a knock on the door.

"Can I help you?" he asked once the couple walked in, completely oblivious to the frustrated tone he was using. He was *hungry*, and that didn't bode well for these people.

"Are you Nick Smith?"

"I am. Can I help you?" he asked again.

"We need your help finding our son-"

"I'm sorry, I'm already booked with cases. I prefer people calling instead of walk-in appointments. Had you called, I would have been able to save you some time." Walk-ins had been happening more and more since the trial earlier that year. Nick had enjoyed it at first- more cases meant more paychecks, after all. But after a few months, it became tiring, especially when most of these people just wanted to hire him because he was on TV that *one time*.

"Please, Mr. Smith. We just drove all the way from Chesapeake to meet with you. Our son- he's been missing for a week. We begged the police to help, but there was no sign of an abduction and they can't do anything else. There's been no contact- he just *vanished*."

"He's only fourteen," the woman sobbed. Nick drummed his thumbs on his desk.

"I'm already working on a missing persons case. I'm worried if I take on another, information will bleed over-"

"Please!" the woman cried. She turned and wept into the man's chest.

"He's just a child. He... He just turned fourteen. Please, Mr. Smith. We'll pay whatever you ask-"

"That's definitely not how I work," Nick said. "I don't extort cases or information for money, especially not when children are involved." He rubbed his face as he considered their request.

Jimmy was fourteen.

He was Nick's world.

Nick couldn't imagine feeling the grief these parents were feeling.

"Please," the father pleaded again, a tear leaking from his eye. Nick nodded, hoping he was making the right decision.

"I need a picture, a name, physical characteristics that aren't seen in pictures, and the last time you saw him." The visible relief the parents showed made Nick feel guilty that he nearly turned them away.

"His name is Rob- Robert Whitten," Nick felt a pang in his chest. He hadn't heard from his brother Robbie in a few weeks. "And he's fourteen. He has a scar on the inside of his left leg from an accident on his bike, and he has a scar on his abdomen from an appendectomy." Nick wrote these notes down on a new sheet of paper.

"And the last time you saw him?"

"Last Wednesday evening. He was going to the school for football practice early Thursday morning. He texted us when he got there, but we haven't heard from him since practice was over. Neither has his coach, nor his friends."

"Ok. Would they be willing to meet with me..." Nick sighed.

"When? They want him found as much as we do."

"Would you mind if I made a phone call? I know most high school football teams are busy on Saturdays, and I am already going to be in Louisa tomorrow. I have a consultant I occasionally employ, but I need to confirm he's available."

"That's fine." Mr. Whitten said. Nick pulled out his cell phone and dialed Mason's number.

"Nicky, I swear-"

"Mason. I need to know if you're available to look into a missing persons case tomorrow in Chesapeake."

"I've got nothing scheduled. I'll get the details tonight."

"Thanks. I'll see what I can have ready for you."

"I thought Jimmy said it was in Louisa?"

"Different case. I'll explain later. Thanks, Dad- Mason." Nick closed his eyes, feeling embarrassed for unknown reasons. He hung up his phone and cleared his throat. "He'll be in Chesapeake tomorrow. I'll send him to your home to view Rob's room. If you could have his friends and maybe even the coach stop by to speak with him? Their parents should be there as well."

"Your father is your consultant?" Mr. Whitten asked with a raised eye.

"He is. He's former FBI and has handled missing children cases before. It's... My brother teaches criminology courses at a university in Florida, my dad is former FBI, and I'm a P.I. Seems to run in the family."

"What's his name? I just want to make sure we know who we're working with, since we were under the impression it would be *you*."

"Mason Johns. He's... He looks like an older version of me, though a bit more gray around the temples and not as... big. He'll be wearing a blue Tar Heels hat, and he will identify himself before he enters your home. And I *will* be looking into this case as well. I had just made other commitments this morning and I can't be there tomorrow. I don't want you and your family to have to wait any longer for me to personally be there. And I assure you, this *will* be a priority."

"Thank you, Mr. Smith," Mrs. Whitten said.

"My son… My son is fourteen. If something happened to him, I would refuse to leave without the promise of help as well." Mr. Whitten nodded.

"May I write down our address and phone number?" Nick nodded and handed them a blank piece of paper.

"Cell phone numbers as well. And here," he said, pulling out a business card. He wrote down Mason's number on the back. "This has my office number, my cell number, and now my father's cell number. If you can think of anything else, please don't hesitate to call. Mason will be there around nine tomorrow morning."

"Thank you, Mr. Smith." Once the information was exchanged, the Whitten's left. Nick sighed and pulled his phone out to call Lucy.

"Hi, you've reached Lucy Smith. I can't answer the phone right now, so please leave a detailed message with your name and number, and I'll get back to you as soon as I can." Nick frowned. Lucy always answered when he called. He quickly shot her a text, apologizing for missing lunch and explaining there was another missing child in Chesapeake. He got up and went to the small kitchen, hoping to find *something* to eat.

Nothing. Nick grabbed his keys and set out to find a quick lunch. He returned as fast as he could with food and took the paper sack back into his office. He typed up as much as he could with one hand until the food was gone- not that it took long with how hungry he was.

"Smith," he answered his ringing phone.

"Hey! Sorry I missed your call. Everything ok?" Lucy asked.

"Yeah. No. Two missing kids. I'll be in Louisa tomorrow and Mason will be in Chesapeake. Of all days for you to have taken off," he smirked into his phone. "I could really use your help-"

"Are you still at the office?"

"I am, but I was kidding, Luce. You never ask to take a day. I'm not going to ask you to come in just because I can't function without you."

"I'd like to stop by as your wife, and not your assistant. Is that ok?"

"Yeah, babe, of course. You don't have to ask. Is everything ok?" The line went dead and Nick stared at his cellphone in disbelief. He waited for Lucy to drop by, pacing in front of his desk. He ran a hand through his hair, trying to get the sudden anxiety to leave him alone.

She hadn't been feeling well.

Cancer? No, the signs weren't there for cancer. Or maybe it was a new type- Nick rubbed his face and tugged at his hair until he heard the car door close. He hurried to the door and threw it open as Lucy walked up to him inside.

"Hi," she said quietly as she closed the door behind her.

"Hi. Lucy, are you ok? You're not acting like yourself. Please..." Lucy met his eye and handed him a glossy picture. Nick gave her a confused look as he brought the picture up.

"I know this wasn't the plan. I'm sorry. We've been safe, but-"

"A baby?" he asked looking at her. "You're having a baby?" Lucy nodded. Nick fell into Lucy's desk chair in disbelief. "A baby."

CHAPTER 4

Mason adjusted his blue Tar Heels hat and looked at the house in front of him. It didn't scream *rich*, but definitely upper middle class. Certainly not something he could have afforded in this area. The water behind the house only added to the expense. All in all, the family was well to do. Why, then, wasn't there a ransom note? Mason walked up to the front door and rang the doorbell. A man close to Nick's age answered the door.

"Can I help you?"

"Good morning. I'm Mason Johns- Nick Smith's consultant. He told me you were expecting me?" Mr. Whitten stepped back and allowed Mason to enter the house.

"Mr. Smith said you were his…"

"Father. Usually he doesn't tell his clients that, so this case must have rattled him. Not that I can blame him. He's very close to his own fourteen year old son." Mason cringed at the sound of crying from another room. "Would you mind showing me to Rob's room?"

"It's this way," Mr. Whitten said. "His friends are going to be here in an hour."

"I'll do what I can in that time, and then work in the room after I talk with the boys as well." Mason followed Mr. Whitten to a room down a hallway. He stepped in and took a deep breath. It reminded him of Jimmy's room- a *bit* childish with burgeoning hints of manhood.

"I can't... I can't stay in here," Mr. Whitten said with a slight quiver in his voice.

"I'll come find you if I have any questions." Mr. Whitten nodded and left, and Mason brought out his mini notebook and pen from his pocket. He made several notes about how organized the room was, especially for a teenage boy. He looked at pictures, titles of books, and a few trophies scattered around the room. Mason even found himself looking under Rob's mattress- that was where he hid his own secrets from his parents, after all. Nothing. There was a laptop at the boy's desk, so he sat in the rolling chair. He opened the computer and was pleasantly surprised there was no password to get on. Then again, Nick told Mason that that was a condition for Jimmy to have his own computer- either no password or Nick was to be given the password. Jimmy had opted for no password.

Mason searched through as many files as he could before the hour was up, but from what he could find, the boy was hiding nothing. It seemed as if the parents' description of Robert being a good boy was actually true instead of wishful thinking or decent deceptive skills by the teen. Mason wondered if this was how Nick and his own Robert would have been as teenagers, and then found himself smirking. No, his boys would have been as bad as he was. Mason felt his phone buzzing and pulled it out.

"Johns."

"Hey. You find anything?"

"Not really. Seemed he was a good kid. Nothing hidden in his computer that I can find. He's got awards for academics and football around the room. I can't even find a skin mag."

"Yeah. Everything is clean here, too. I've got nothing, Dad, and I don't like it. I'm wondering if the cops are right-"

"This kid was the star JV running back. He had more going for him here than running away. And I can't find anything, either, but I can't just go tell his parents that."

"So what do we do? This girl was working on getting her license. I'm looking at the workbook from the DMV. She wouldn't have just gone, either. But I can't..."

"Can't what, Nicky?"

"I can't string them along if I've got nothing. Not like what that guy did to you about us." Mason took a breath and slowly let it out, trying to think of a solution.

"Ok. It's Friday. Let's work on it during the weekend and if by Sunday night we still have nothing, we'll... turn it over to Thomas." Mason heard the scoffing. "It's the best I got, kid."

"Yeah. Yeah, alright. I guess if that's the best we got, then that's just going to have to be good enough for now."

"I'm sorry. I've never seen a case like this, and now there's two, nearly identical to each other." Mason frowned at the silence. "Nicky?"

"They are really similar, aren't they?"

"A coincidence, I'm sure-"

"Is anything ever a coincidence when it comes to things like this, Mason? Can you just..."

"Give me some questions to ask and I will, son."

"I don't know. Kids aren't my... These hit a little closer to home. Even Mom's case wasn't this- I've got to go. Abby's friends are showing up. Just... I don't know, Dad. Write down whatever questions you ask and we'll compare them later, I suppose."

"Ok. Be careful Nick. Love you."

"Yeah. Me too, Dad." Mason hung up and rubbed his face. He was worried about his son. Nick was never this scattered. He could barely form coherent sentences the previous night, and that was before the single beer he took three hours to drink.

"Mr. Johns?" Mason turned and saw a young black haired girl. "Some of Rob's friends are here. My mom sent me to get you."

"Thank you. What's your name?"

"Julie."

"Hi, Julie. You can call me Mason, if you'd like."

"My dad says that's rude." Mason chuckled.

"Usually it is, unless you're told by the person you're talking to that it's fine. Even my sons call me Mason sometimes."

"Really?"

"Really. Can you show me where I'm supposed to go?"

"Sure. They're in the den." Mason followed Julie out of Rob's room and to a room off the side of the kitchen, wondering if he and Jenny's unborn baby had been a girl. He'd always wanted a little girl. One who looked just like- Mason rolled his shoulders and shook his head. It wasn't the time or place to let his mind drift.

"Ah. Mr. Johns-"

"Mason, please," he said with a smile to the woman.

"Mason," she said with a small nod. "These are Rob's friends: Ben, Devon, and Jase." Mason sat in a recliner and motioned the boys to the couch across from him. He took a moment to study the teens. One of the boys reminded him of a shorter Jimmy- brown hair and green eyes. Another seemed a bit tanner- Pacific Islander, possibly? And the third boy was dark skinned.

"Please. Have a seat. Did none of your parents want to come?" The boys looked at each other before turning back to Mason. The boy with the tanned skin seemed to be elected their speaker as he took a deep breath before addressing Mason.

"They all work. They..."

"They what?" Mason prodded.

"They think Rob took off," the boy admitted.

"He wouldn't have-"

"Mrs. Whitten, please. I'm sure Rob wouldn't be just a runaway, but I need to know what *others* are saying as well."

"Would it be better if I stepped out?" Mason looked at the teens in front of him.

"I think it might be a good idea. Would you mind getting these young men something to drink?" She nodded and walked out. "Ok. You boys are hiding something, I can tell."

"We don't want him to get in trouble," one of the boys, the dark skinned one, said. Mason felt relieved. Answers, finally.

"His parents are worried sick. Enough so that the private investigator that they *hired* to find him employed *me*, a retired FBI agent. So let's hear it."

"It was after practice-" the boy who reminded Mason of Jimmy started to say.

"Shut up, Jase. He just said he was FBI-"

"*Former.* Jase. Please continue." Mason gave a look to the tanned skinned boy, hoping he wouldn't be interrupted again.

"It's not that big a deal-"

"This investigator isn't cheap, boys, and I charge a pretty penny, too. Rob's parents are paying for every *hour* I'm here. Now, while this doesn't bother me, I'm sure eventually it will bother them. So get talking *now*," he said, ending in a growl. Even his stubborn Nick obeyed when he used *that* voice.

"It was after practice," Jase said again. "This

guy pulled up in a truck and Rob seemed to know him. He told us he'd see us the next day, but…"

"I need to know *everything* you three noticed about that car. This isn't a time to hold information back, boys. If the police knew you'd withheld this, there could be a lot of problems. Got me?"

"Yes sir. It was a dark green truck." Mason nodded as he wrote down the information.

"Make, model? One of you has to be a car guy. Come on."

"I think it was a Chevy?" Jase said.

"You think, or you *know*? This is extremely important-"

"I couldn't see a make. Why?"

"Because now that I have this, it looks more like your friend was *kidnapped.* So I need whatever you can give me so I can either go to the police or contact my friends at the FBI. What can you tell me about the driver? Old, young? Black, white, Hispanic, Asian?"

"He was like our parents' age. And white, but I guess he could have been Asian, too," the third boy, Devon, spoke up.

"Did you see his hair? Eye color-?"

"He had a hat on. It was red. And he was wearing sunglasses."

"A hat and sunglasses?" Mason confirmed.

"Yeah. I remember thinking how weird it was."

"Perfect. What else?"

"Rob knew him," Jase said with a shrug. "We didn't think it was that big of a deal."

"Unfortunately, you're more likely to be kidnapped by someone you know over someone you don't. The person you know has already a level of trust-" Mason stopped at the terrified looks the boys were giving him. "You should take a drink from Mrs. Whitten to not be rude, and then you should head home." Mason stood and walked out of the room, texting Nick to call him as soon as he could.

"Mason? Would you like some lemonade?" Mason turned and looked at Julie. He gave her a small smile.

"I'd love some, thank you." She handed him a glass with a smile. Mason took a sip and fought not to make a face, wondering if Lucy had given this family whatever cup of sugar she'd used in Jimmy's cake the night before.

"Mason? The boys said you were sending them home. Is everything ok?"

"Mrs. Whitten, I'd like to speak with you and your husband. Privately."

"They know something."

"Mrs. Whitten," Mason said again, using his head to gesture to Julie.

"Please, follow me. Julie, go to your room, dear." Mason watched her scamper away and he followed Mrs. Whitten to the room with the front door.

"Mr. Johns?" Mr. Whitten said, standing

from the chair he'd been sitting in. "Do you have a question?"

"The boys seemed to be under the impression that Rob got into a truck with someone after that last practice. Do you know anyone with a truck?"

"You're kidding, right?" Mr. Whitten scoffed. "*Everyone* owns a truck these days. Hell, *I* own a truck."

"Anyone that Rob would feel comfortable enough to get a ride home with?"

"No."

"Are you saying he was kidnapped?" Mason took a deep breath.

"It's what everything is pointing towards right now. I'm sorry. I'm happy to alert the local police-"

"No-"

"Tina!"

"They couldn't find anything! He's been here all of what, less than two hours? Yet he already has more information-"

"How do we know it's *real* and not a ploy for money? It's for his son, after all." Mason glared, insulted that that's what they thought of both him and his son.

"I've never lied or made things up for my son's benefit. *You* asked for his help. This is him giving it. You can either take it and go to the police, or ignore it and find a P.I. who'll drain your accounts while not looking for your son."

"He couldn't even be bothered to come himself-"

"Because he wanted to help immediately instead of making you wait until Monday. He was already obligated to go to a woman in Louisa County whose daughter is missing, just like your son." Mason pulled his hat down and pulled out his keys. "You have my number and his number. Please let us know what you decide." He knew if they refused to call the police, he'd call his former second in command, SSA Russell Thomas. Mason let himself out of the house and went to his car.

CHAPTER 5

Nick looked at his phone after he felt the slight buzz. Seeing it was a text from Mason, he ignored it and continued to listen to the story from Veronica.

"And you didn't see her at all?" he asked the brown skinned girl.

"No. She texted me that she was going to get a ride from one of her mom's friends, but that was the last I heard."

"You didn't tell the police?"

"I *did*, Mr. Smith. As soon as Ms. Fran asked if I'd seen Abby. I knew something was wrong and we went to the police. They told us it sounded like a classic runaway case and to give her time to come home." Nick shook his head.

"I can't imagine. Usually everything is dropped for children." Nick sighed. "Can you think of *anything* else, Ronnie? Even if it doesn't seem important."

"No. Abby was the good girl. She did her homework, she kept in contact with her mom, she wouldn't even sneak into an 'R' movie, Mr. Smith. She was- everything was black and white, good and bad, you know?"

"Not personally," Nick smirked. "But I know the type. Ok. Thank you for your time, Ronnie. I really appreciate it. Fran has my number, so if you think of something, let me know. I don't care if it hits you at two in the morning, ok? Finding Abby is the most important thing."

"Ok, Mr. Smith. Thank you for looking for her." Nick nodded to her and to her mother before standing.

"Anything?" Mrs. Hannen asked.

"She said Abby told her she got a ride with one of your friends."

"I don't… I don't have many friends here. We've kept to ourselves, mostly."

"From what I've learned about your daughter, she wouldn't have just climbed in the car with a stranger. So if she *did* get a ride with someone, it would make sense that she knew the driver."

"I'm sorry, Nick. I don't have an answer for you." Nick sighed and looked around the small room.

"How long have you lived in this area?" He asked, confused about the lack of adult friends for Mrs. Hannen. Even he had a couple friends. Granted, he married one and the other sold him beers at the bar he frequented, but *still*.

"Nearly all of Abby's life. She and Ronnie met in preschool and have been inseparable since."

"Where were you before Louisa?"

"Near Farmville. I met my husband in college. We moved here because he wanted the safety of a small town," she sniffed. "Now I've lost them both."

"You can't think like that," Nick said, sternly. "The minute you give up, she *is* gone. You *have* to believe she'll come home-"

"She wasn't a runaway!"

"No, I don't think she was, either, Mrs. Hannen. I don't know your daughter, but from looking through her things… Abby said several times how happy she was that she still had you, and that she was going to make something of herself to repay you for everything you had to give up. She wouldn't write that and then *run*."

"Thank you."

"I'm going to do another sweep of the house. Is that ok?"

"Whatever you need to do to find her." Nick nodded and started looking around the living room again. He pulled his phone back out and saw the text from Mason asking him to call immediately. He dialed the number and held the phone to his ear.

"Hey. So Rob's friends talked about how he got a ride with someone after practice, and he hasn't been seen since. This was about a week ago."

"That's… Abby's friend said she texted her that she was getting a ride from her mom's friend to the theater. That was Sunday. She was reported missing a few hours later."

"Nicky…"

"I don't like the sound of it, either, Dad. Two families, several hundred miles away, same story?

No… There's got to be a connection. Maybe…"

"*Maybe what, kid?*"

"Her mom's friend. Mrs. Hannen said she's originally from Farmville. I wonder…"

"*You'll have to reach out, Nick. They weren't too happy with me. Accused me of making something up to get you paid more money.*"

"Great. Alright. I'll give them a call in a minute. Did the kids happen to see-?"

"*Look, I'm driving. I'll get to the office and start typing shit up for you to go over later, alright? We'll talk when you get in.*"

"Yeah." Nick sighed and rubbed his head.

"*Nicky? What's wrong?*"

"Why would you ask that?"

"*Because you're not acting like yourself-*"

"You've known me for-"

"*You act like I don't know my own son.*"

"I don't think this is an appropriate time for a heart to heart, Mason."

"*Ok. I'll get my answer, though, Nick. I'm good at finding things out.*"

"Unless-"

"*Nope. Don't go there. I'll see you in a few hours.*" The line went dead and Nick slid his phone in his pocket. He took a few more minutes to look around before realizing there was nothing new he could find.

"Mrs. Hannen?"

"Yes?"

"I think I've gotten everything I could from

here. I have a few pages of notes I've written down that I need to go over with my consultant. I'm going to head back to my office and do what I can from there."

"Are you sure?"

"Yes ma'am. But if I have any questions-"

"Please call me."

"Thank you. And please call me if there's anything you can think of. Here," Nick said, pulling out a business card. He wrote down Mason's number on the back. "This is my consultant's cell number. If I don't answer my office phone or my cell, he should. And I'm usually with him-"

"The two of you can't work nonstop, Nick," she admonished in a motherly tone, despite being nearly the same age as Nick.

"We do what needs to be done," Nick told her. "And it's not... Mason Johns is actually my father as well as my consultant, so he's usually visiting my son when we're not working."

"He must be proud of all of the good things you've done."

"That's what he says," Nick said with a small smile. "I'm going to head back now. Please call or text me if you can think of anything, ok?"

"I will." Nick nodded to her and walked out of the house to his motorcycle. He put his Tar Heels hat in his side bag, secured his shoulder bag, and put on his helmet before starting it up and zooming off.

CHAPTER 6

"So, two kids are missing from different cities in Virginia, but both kids' friends say they got in their parents' friend's truck?" Jimmy asked at the table that night.

"Looks that way," Nick told him, picking at his dinner. Lucy watched him in concern, but didn't want to say anything in front of Jimmy.

"So what are you and Grandpa going to do about it?"

"I don't know. There's not a lot of information out there… I know Mason said if the family in Chesapeake refuses to say anything to the police, he's calling Russell."

"What about the lady in Louisa?"

"She's been annoying the police every day asking if they've heard something. I'm not concerned about her not giving them more information."

"Do you think it's the same guy?"

"Hard to say." Nick rubbed his face. "I think I'm going to call it an early night. Mason and I are going to be busy this weekend." Nick stood up and took his plate into the small kitchen, returned to kiss the top of Jimmy's head, and headed back to his room.

"Is he ok?" Jimmy asked Lucy.

"He's just…"

"Lucy. I'm not a kid anymore." Lucy gave her stepson an indulgent smile.

"You'll always be a kid to your dad, Jimmy."

"He's not acting right. He hasn't been since yesterday."

"I think he's just rattled. One of the missing kids reminds him of you."

"Oh." Jimmy started picking at his own dinner. "Are you guys hiding something from me?"

"What?"

"He did this when he proposed and didn't tell me."

"Jimmy,"

"You aren't getting divorced, are you?"

"What? No, Jimmy. Your dad and I are still very happy together."

"Is Grandpa ok? What about Uncle Robbie? I know Dad's worried about him- I think he forgets he's a professor and school starts in August."

"As far as I know, everyone is fine. Look, Jimmy. If you're concerned about something-"

"I'm concerned about my dad and it seems like I'm the only one." Jimmy stood up and put his plate in the sink. "I'm going to start looking over my schedule for the semester." Jimmy left Lucy and went back to his room, closing the door loud enough to show his irritation without slamming it to invoke Nick's wrath. Lucy sighed and put her own plate in the dishwasher, adding Nick and Jimmy's to the dishwasher as well. She started organizing things in the living room and picking up random socks the two males had left lying around. Once she was satisfied with the room, she made her way back to her and Nick's bedroom. Nick was on his side under the blankets.

"Nick?"

"Yeah?" he responded in a flat voice.

"Jimmy's noticing something. We should tell him-"

"I can't right now, Lucy. I can't…"

"Are you that against our baby?"

"Lucy, I had a vasectomy when Jimmy was a newborn. That's not my baby. Which means either someone attacked you and you didn't tell me, or there's someone else." Lucy sat next to Nick and put a hand on him, which he quickly shrugged off. He got out of the bed and started pacing.

"I've never cheated on you, Nick."

"Then how the hell-?"

"I don't know. But it might have been nice to know you had a *vasectomy* before we got married."

"I was clear with you that Jimmy was *it* for me-"

"Well, I don't know what to tell you, Nick, but this is *definitely* your baby. And if you don't believe me, then… Mason has a spare room." Nick looked at her, shocked.

"You're kicking me out?!"

"Only if you'd actually believe I'd cheat on you!"

"You had to get pregnant somehow!" Lucy

stood and glared at him.

"I'll call Mason and ask him to get a room ready." She walked out of the room.

"Lucy. Lucy!" Nick called, following her out of their room.

"Dad?" Jimmy said, stepping into the hall.

"Everything is fine, Jim. Go back to your room."

"But-"

"Room!" Nick sighed as he felt his phone buzzing and heard Jimmy's door slam shut. He saw Mason calling and he let out a frustrated growl as he answered it. "What?"

"*Lucy said you needed a night away?*"

"Well, apparently Lucy knows everything-"

"*Watch your mouth, boy. That's your wife.*" Nick felt his irritation blossom into near rage.

"Did she tell you what was going on?"

"*Nope. I'll see you in ten, Nick.*" Nick threw his phone on his bed and ran a hand through his hair.

"Go, Nick." He spun around and saw Lucy at the doorway.

"My *son* is here-"

"And I'll drop him off tomorrow if you want him. Must be nice for him. I don't know what I'll tell this baby." Nick grabbed his shoulder bag and stuffed some clothes inside. He left the room and took his keys off the hook before leaving, slamming the door behind him. He hopped on his motorcycle and took off towards Mason's house, not bothering with his helmet in his frustration.

Once there, he stormed up the sidewalk and pounded on the door. Mason answered, eye raised.

"You need to calm down."

"She's cheating on *me* and *I* need to calm down?!" Mason blinked and opened the door wider for Nick to come in.

"Is that what's been bothering you?" Nick threw himself on the couch and put his head in his hands.

"She's pregnant."

"Nick, that's great. Congratulations-"

"I had a vasectomy when Jimmy was little, before Carol..." Nick wiped his face. "It's not my baby." Mason sighed.

"Want a beer?"

"I don't think I should drink right now."

"I'll keep you in the house and take your phone so you don't do anything stupid." Mason went into the kitchen and brought a beer back to Nick as well as one for himself.

"I never thought she'd do this to me. I know I'm not the easiest person to get along with, but..." Nick wiped at his face.

"So what are you going to do?"

"I don't know. She's refusing to admit it. But the proof..." Nick took a sip of his beer, not wanting to say any more on the subject.

"You know those aren't always..." Mason scratched his head. "They don't always take."

"What?"

"There was a case I did a few years ago. Guy

raped several girls, thought he'd be fine without a rubber. Six of them got pregnant from him."

"You can't know that-"

"He had a thing for virgins."

"The pamphlet said it could take a few months-"

"It had been four years since his."

"Years?" Dread filled Nick's chest as he wondered just how badly he had screwed up things with his wife.

"Yeah. We talked to a bunch of doctors, did our own research. Depending on the type done, sometimes things... heal. Makes the procedure useless."

"Oh God," Nick said, flopping back on the couch as he threw his hand over his face.

"You might want to grovel and get checked, son."

"I can't... She has every reason to leave me." Nick dragged his hand over his face and dropped it in his lap.

"I don't think she will. I think she kicked you out to make sure nothing was said that was irreparable. But I'd be willing to bet that she's crushed, Nicky. She's done so much for you as your assistant, your girlfriend, your *wife*. She works with you, son. When would she have even found the *time*?"

"I don't know," he said quietly. "I left my phone at home. Can I...?" Mason handed Nick his phone, patted his shoulder, and stepped out of the room. Nick wiped at his face again before dialing Lucy's number.

"Mason? Is he ok?" Nick closed his eyes at the clear concern in Lucy's voice.

"It's me. Lucy-"

"Unless you're apologizing-"

"I am. I said some pretty rough things, and… Lucy, I'm sorry."

"I would never cheat on you, Nick. I can't believe you'd even think that."

"In my defense-"

"You have no defense!" Nick closed his eyes and took a breath.

"As far as I knew, I couldn't have any more kids. Suddenly you show up pregnant. What was I supposed to think, Lucy? Because in my mind, cheating was more likely than me suddenly producing sperm again."

"And now?"

"Mason…" Nick rubbed his face. "I didn't know that it could fail years after, Lucy. I was warned about weeks and a few months, but not *years."*

"So you believe me now?"

"I believe there's a chance my vasectomy failed, and I believe you'd never cheat on me. Putting them together… Jimmy's going to be a big brother." Nick shook his head. "At least we have a free sitter at the house."

"You're… happy?"

"Yeah. And I'm sorry, babe. I should have…

I never should have let my head go there. I won't blame you if you don't forgive me."

"It'll take some time, Nick."

"I'm sorry." The line went dead and Nick put the phone on the couch next to him.

"Didn't take it so well, did she?" Nick looked up and glared at Mason.

"What do *you* think?"

"I think you need to get some sleep before you say something and get kicked out of my house, too." Nick rubbed his eyes.

"I've never been in the doghouse this bad."

"Flowers. Chocolate. Diamonds."

"Oh, because you'd know how to-"

"I *was* married, Nicky," Mason said softly. "And you inherited my stubborn temper."

"I didn't think you and Mom fought." Mason chuckled and moved to sit beside Nick.

"We started dating in high school, kid. Married right after basic training. There were two years before you came along. Worst fight we had was when you were nearly three and I re-enlisted without talking to her first. I thought for sure she was going to leave me. I was on the couch for nearly the whole month I was home."

"How did you get her to forgive you?" Mason shrugged.

"I stepped up at home, let her relax. Took you out a lot. Came home with flowers, both from a florist and from yards. She never wanted jewelry from *me*, so I took you to the store and *you* picked something out for her."

"I did?" Mason nodded.

"It was the *ugliest* necklace I'd ever seen. But she was so proud. She wore it as often as she could because you saw it and thought she'd like it."

"How long did it take for her to forgive you?" Nick asked, soaking up as much about his mother as he could. He was grateful Mason never teased him about that- everything else, sure, but anything about Jenny... Mason just seemed happy to finally have someone to talk to about his late wife.

"Not long after that." Mason chuckled. "Robbie came nine months later," he winked.

"I really could have gone the rest of my life without knowing that."

"Just... Grovel, Nicky. And then be ready to grovel for the rest of your life."

"Great." Mason squeezed Nick's arm and stood.

"I should get to bed. I've got a boss who's an ass about being on time, and he wants me in on a *Saturday* at eight."

"Hm. Maybe bring in breakfast. Bet he'd be less grumpy," Nick smirked.

"I'll consider it. I'll just have to forgo the coffee. Heard he likes to spill it everywhere." Nick felt his face heating up as Mason walked down the hall, laughing.

CHAPTER 7

Nick and Mason had been pouring over their notes, and each other's notes, for several hours that following Saturday morning. They agreed with their initial thoughts: the two missing children were not kids who would just 'run away.'

"You know this means we need to contact the police, right? We don't have the manpower for this," Nick told Mason, close to noon. "My pride won't let *kids* suffer. I can't..."

"No, I agree. You get Louisa, I'll get Chesapeake." Nick nodded and looked up the non-emergency line for the Louisa County Sheriff's Department.

"Louisa County Sheriff's office."

"Good afternoon, my name is Nick Smith. I'm a private investigator hired by-"

"Did Mrs. Hannen hire you?"

"Yes, she did," Nick replied with narrowed eyes.

"Mr. Smith, her daughter ran away-"

"No, she didn't," Nick said, now glaring at his wall. "I have been through the girl's personal effects, I have spoken with her friends, and I have come to the conclusion that this girl was *kidnapped* nearly a week ago!"

"I know you might think this, but with the lack

of evidence-"

"Her friend said she was getting a ride to a theater with a friend of her mom's-"

"Exactly. She was safe. We watched the footage, Mr. Smith. She willingly climbed into the car-"

"Her mom doesn't have any friends in the area!"

"And you know this how, Mr. Smith?"

"Because I was doing *your* damn job! There is a missing *child* and you have just been waiting on information to fall into your lap instead of looking! You tossed her aside as a runaway! You had *no* reason to think that but you... If something happens to this girl, I will hire the best attorney and I will make sure you and your entire department pay for ignoring a *child*." Nick hung up and tossed his phone on the desk, fuming.

"Sounds about how it went for me." Nick looked up and saw Mason.

"You look as pissed as when you thought I killed Mom." Mason snorted.

"They're adamant the kid just ran. There's no evidence to support a kidnapping, but they have patrol cars canvassing the area. That's the best they can do without more information." Nick ran a hand through his hair.

"I can't... They're *kids*, Dad. *Why*?"

"I don't know, Nick. I'll call Russ-" The bell over the door rang and Nick looked up.

"Mr. Smith?" A brown haired, bespectacled

man asked, coming into the office. A weeping woman was with him, holding onto a young adult male who looked like the older man he was with.

"Yes? Can I help you?"

"My... Our daughters, Mr. Smith. They're twins- just twelve years old."

"Please don't... Missing?" *Shit*, Nick thought. If they were missing-

"They went missing on Wednesday. They're *twelve*. The police are saying they ran because there's no evidence saying other-"

"Mason, I need you to get them here *now*." Mason nodded and pressed something on his phone before holding it to his ear.

"I don't understand. What's going on?" The man asked.

"You're the third set of parents coming to me and asking me for help with a missing child, children in your case. Please. Their names, pictures- anything you think that might be helpful."

"Wendy and Rahne-" Nick bit his tongue at the names- Windy and Rain?- "Fredericks. They're twelve. Brown hair, green eyes- identical twins. They were supposed to come home after a birthday party. My son got there to bring them home and he was told that they'd already been picked up."

"Did anyone see the car?" Mason asked, phone moved away from his mouth.

"A green truck," the boy answered.

"Nick."

"Yeah, I know. Mr. Fredericks, is there anyone you know who drives a green truck?"

"No. We... we're new in the area-Charlottesville."

"Where did you live before this?"

"Farmville. We were both born and raised there." Nick's head popped up from writing down the notes.

"You said Farmville?"

"I did. Is that... Is that a problem?"

"Do you know a Frances Hannen?"

"Y-yes. But we knew her as Frances Simmons. We went to high school together."

"Were you friends with her?"

"Yes? Why? You don't think she-"

"Her daughter is missing. What about Richard Whitten, or Tina Whitten?"

"Richard, definitely. We were all friends- *best* friends, in fact," Mr. Fredericks explained.

"Mr. Fredericks, I need the names of your high school friends, now."

"Um, Fran, Richard, the two of us- Geoffry with a 'G' and Diana-, Damien Kingaly, and Michael Wood. We were nearly inseparable in high school, and then we all went our own ways after graduation. I haven't... We lost communication until social media, but we hadn't seen them until our 25th reunion this past May."

"Ok. The two kids who went missing before your twins were seen, or told their friends they were getting in a car with a friend of their parents. We had no… Your daughters aren't runaways, I can tell you that for certain." Mrs. Fredericks began wailing into the chest of the young man.

"What do we do?" Mr. Fredericks asked.

"I'm on the phone with the FBI," Mason said.

"Does he have you on hold?"

"Only to get the team together. Don't start that crap about Feds right now, Nick."

"I need to reach out to your other friends. Do either of them have kids?"

"Uh- Damien does. I don't think Mike does, though."

"No, he does. She's ten or eleven."

"Then I need to contact Damien and Mike immediately. Do you have their numbers?"

"No. Like I said, until social media-"

"Then I need you to send them a message. We can see that it's the same thing happening to all four kids, and now there's a connection between the three families. Ask them to contact me and give them my number. Please." Mr. Fredericks nodded and pulled out his phone.

"I sent it."

"Team's on the way," Mason said, putting his phone down.

"Good. We need all the help we can get." Mason raised an eye.

"That's it?"

"There are kids involved." Mason nodded his acceptance of Nick's agreement of the FBI coming as Nick's phone rang. Nick saw the number was unrecognized and quickly answered it. "Hello?"

"Hi, is this… Nick? My friend Geoff said it was important I called you."

"Is this Mr. Kingaly or Mr. Wood?"

"I'm Damien Kingaly."

"Mr. Kingaly, I'm Nick Smith, a private investigator. I've been approached by three families about their children going missing. We had no link until today, and that link is that at least one person in each family attended high school together. Now this is very important: do you live in Virginia, and do you know where your child is?"

"Uh- her mother took her to Texas for a week to visit her parents. And yes, I live in Virginia. Do you think my daughter is in danger?"

"It's a possibility. I need you to keep a lookout for a green truck. It's been seen at two of the three abduction sites. Please call me if you see it, and I'd recommend keeping your daughter away from Virginia."

"I'll inform her mother. Thank you, Mr. Smith." Nick hung up and his phone started buzzing immediately again.

"Nick Smith."

"Mr. Smith, this is Mike Wood. I was told to reach out to you?"

"Yes, Mr. Wood. I'm a private investigator-"

"And I'll stop you there. Yes, I know where my ex is, no I don't want to see her. She gave up her rights to our daughter-"

"No, I'm investigating three different abductions of four children. We were informed today that the parents of these children were friends in high school, and you were named in their group. I'm just trying to reach out to make sure your child is safe, and that she stays that way."

"Oh my- Oh my God. Uh- yeah. I'll keep an eye out. Thanks. Do you know what I need to look out for?"

"There's a green truck. And that the children seem to think it's a friend of their parents from school. The entire group Mr. Fredericks mentioned has children, so I don't think... I believe it's someone who tried to insert his or herself in your group but didn't quite make it."

"Why now?"

"Mr. Fredericks said something about a reunion in May. But everything else is speculation on my end. I have contacts coming from the FBI and they should help narrow down the 'why's' better than what I can do right now."

"Thank you, Mr. Smith. I'll reach out to the other parents who attended the reunion and warn them as well."

"That would be appreciated. Thank you." Nick hung up and looked at the family in front of him.

"What can we do?"

"Go get some lunch," Mason suggested after seeing Nick rubbing his eyes. "The FBI will want to talk to you, and we'll need to get the other families here as well. I'd look into a hotel room, too. If this guy's moving all over Virginia, there's…" Mason took a breath. "My team will be able to tell you where to go from there."

"Thank you," Mr. Fredericks said as he stood. He led his family out and Nick looked at Mason.

"Now what do we do?"

"We wait for Russ and the team to get here and follow their lead."

"I'm not big on following-"

"Kid, I will kick your ass if you give them a hard time."

"Mason!"

"I won't have you embarrassing me-"

"I'm forty-"

"Then you'll act like it," Mason said, giving Nick a pointed look.

"I need to go home and let Lucy know what's going on." Nick grabbed his keys and started walking out.

"Bring back some lunch!" Mason called after him.

CHAPTER 8

"At least you have something to work with now," Lucy said, rubbing Jimmy's shoulders.

"Yeah. Russ should be here soon with the team."

"Can I see them, Dad? I haven't seen Betty since-"

"A month ago?" Nick said, eye raised. Jimmy blushed.

"She's like a cool aunt."

"Mmhm."

"Nick," Lucy said. "Should we...?" She gave Nick a pointed look and then looked at Jimmy.

"You *are* keeping something from me!" Nick looked at Lucy, who nodded.

"Jim... Why don't we talk on the way to the office?"

"Why don't we talk now?" Jimmy asked, crossing his arms.

"Why don't you watch how you talk to me before I put you over my knee?"

"Nick," Lucy chided.

"Jimmy, I won't say it again. Get your stuff and get to the car."

"Jackass," Jimmy muttered as he turned.

"James Robert-" Nick said as he grabbed the back of Jimmy's shirt.

"Nick-" Nick let him go and Jimmy went down the hall, eager to escape Nick for the moment.

"He's not going to talk to me like that!"

"Then quit treating me like a child!" Jimmy yelled from his room.

"You *are* a child!" Jimmy came back to the room with a backpack slung over his shoulder.

"You treat me more like a kid now than you did when I was *twelve!*"

"Excuse me for wanting you to enjoy the last few years you have before-"

"This isn't how this is supposed to be happening!" Lucy said with tears in his eyes. Nick quickly deflated.

"I'm sorry. Jimmy... I'll tell you everything, but I've got to get back to work. Please come with me?"

"You've got to stop threatening to... do that to me."

"I will when Mason stops threatening me," Nick muttered. Jimmy smirked at the thought of his imposing father being chastised like a child. Nick went to kiss Lucy, but she turned her head. Nick blinked away the hurt and kissed her cheek instead. "I love you."

"Go to work, Nick."

"I'll be back in a few hours," he promised. He led Jimmy to the car and they started driving to the office.

"She promised."

"What?"

"Lucy said you weren't getting a divorce."

"We're not. We're just…" Nick sighed. "I said some things and she's upset, rightfully so."

"About what?"

"Lucy's pregnant. And I accused her of being with someone else to get that way."

"You really *are* a jackass!"

"Jimmy!"

"Lucy loves you! She'd never-"

"I *know*! I… I messed up and I'm taking my licks, Jim, ok? So if you could just not make this harder on me, I'd appreciate it. And watch your language- you're fourteen." Jimmy sighed and leaned against the window.

"Ok," he said after a few moments of silence. "How far along is she?"

"Due in March."

"Do you know what it is?"

"No. We won't for a few months." Nick parked at his office and saw unknown cars. "I never thought I'd have to work with them again."

"It'll be fine."

"Yeah… Once they take over and kick me off the case, you feel like helping me with something?"

"What?"

"I need to get a peace offering gift for Lucy. Was hoping you'd have an idea of what I could do."

"Well she's already pregnant-" Nick gently slapped Jimmy's head.

"Watch your mouth." Jimmy just smirked and climbed out of the car. Nick cut the engine and did the same. He put his hand on Jimmy's shoulder and led him into the office.

"There they are. Geez, Nick. You were supposed to be gone ten minutes, not *forty*."

"Afternoon delight, Smith?" SSA Russell Thomas said with a smirk.

"You only take forty minutes?" Nick returned.

"Dad!" Jimmy exclaimed, face turning red.

"Get your stuff in the office, kid."

"Where's lunch?" Mason asked as Jimmy headed into Nick's office.

"Just order some pizza or Chinese. Use my card." Mason smirked as Nick handed him his credit card. He looked at his former team and its new members, holding the card up between two fingers.

"You guys hungry? Kid's buying."

"Damn it, Mason!"

"Just order some pizza, Grandpa. Dad's taking me out later to get an apology gift for Lucy, and I plan to make sure it's expensive." Mason chuckled and rubbed Jimmy's hair.

"Family life looks good on you, Mase."

"Feels good," Mason told Russell. "Betty. How's this guy treating you?"

"Definitely not you, but nothing to complain about. Yet. Nick, how's Lucy? What are you apologizing for?"

"She's... Why don't you stop by the house for dinner? I'll let her complain about me," Nick told her with a wry grin.

"Let's see what this investigation requires from us first, Mr. Smith." Nick turned and looked towards the feminine voice he didn't recognize.

"Who are you?"

"Agent Green."

"Agent Green. You could be a bit nicer in my office. We didn't have to call you, you know." Nick looked around. "Russ, where's Josh?"

"That's SSA Thomas-"

"That's my dad's former partner."

"He's fine, Green. Agent Miller was transferred to New York," Russell told Nick.

"That's too bad-"

"No, he was looking forward to it. Most of his family's there."

"Then good for him."

"We can catch up later, Smith. Mason told us some of what's going on. Can you fill us in the rest of the way?"

"Three families have come to me asking for help-"

"From *you*?" Nick flashed a look of pure hatred towards Agent Green.

"Russ, I'm going to give her one more chance, and then she's out of my office."

"Green. Smith here is who caught Phil Anderson last summer. He's plenty capable. Nick, please continue."

"I went to the first woman's house in Louisa County yesterday. Mason went to Chesapeake to the other family. Both families were told by the police that since there were no ransom notes, the kids were just runaways so they wouldn't look into it. The friends of the missing kids had similar stories- Abby Hannen's friend said she texted her about getting a ride from her mom's friend, and Rob Whitten's friends said he said the same thing, and they saw him climb into a green truck. This morning-"

"Noon," Mason corrected. "It was just after twelve."

"This *afternoon*," Nick said, rolling his eyes, "another family came in saying their twins were missing. Brother went to pick them up from a party and witnesses said they got in a green truck after saying it was their parents' friend."

"Ok," Russ said, writing the information down. "What made you connect them?"

"Abby Hannen's mom said something about being from Farmville, Geoff Fredericks said he was from Farmville as well. Knowing how small the city is," Nick ignored the scoff from Agent Green, "I thought to ask if they knew each other. They did. All three families- Frances Hannen, Richard Whitten, and Geoff and Diana Fredericks went to high school together. Not only that, but they were all really good friends- they were a clique of sorts. These kidnappings didn't start until this month, but there *was* a high school reunion in May they attended. I think whoever is doing this was there and is jealous-"

"Now he's a profiler, too?" Agen Green sneered.

"Lady, would you just be *quiet*?" Nick's lips quirked up in a small smile before forcing it off his face.

"Jim."

"What? The Nick Smith of two years ago wouldn't put up with this!" Nick just pointed to Mason while looking at his son with a raised eye.

"You said the third family came today?" Betty asked, trying to get the conversation back on the case.

"Yes. Mason sent them out for lunch and to wait for you."

"Alright. Green, go with Martin to Chesapeake to interview the family there. Smith has their address. Wilson, you and Lang drive to Louisa and talk to that family. I'll stay and see the family here." Nick and Mason passed out the addresses and phone numbers of the families, as well as copies of their notes for the two cases.

"Thanks, Nick," Betty said. "I'll probably need a raincheck on dinner."

"You should give her a call, then. She'd probably love to vent about how I screwed up."

"I'll see what I can do."

"Here," Nick said, handing Betty the laptop from his bag. "This is Abby's laptop. Her mom… You should look through it on the way there."

"Thanks." Betty took the laptop, motioned to the only other agent Nick was unfamiliar with, and the two left the office.

"Will you need anything from me, Russ?"

"Your notes from the third case?"

"On my desk."

"You good if I copy them?"

"Have at it," Nick said. "I trust *you*. But that Agent Green..."

"Don't get me started. I prefer you, don't worry. *Pre* Mason straightening you out, too."

"She must be horrible," Mason quipped. Nick flipped his father off.

"Dad has a key, so lock up when you're done if I'm not back yet."

"Thanks, Smith."

"Yeah, yeah. Getting soft in my old age."

"Apparently not that soft," Mason smirked.

"My *kid* is here!" Nick said, dramatically covering Jimmy's ears.

"Can we go before *another* joke is made? Please?" Nick gave Jimmy the car keys and sent him out.

"Seriously- call me or text me with updates. I know I'm *off* the case-"

"We can take you on as a consultant again," Russ offered.

"That would mean I would have to work with Agent PMS." Russell chuckled and Mason rolled his eyes.

"I'll keep you two apart. If I remember,

you're partial to Betty-"

"Be careful saying things like that," Nick said sternly. Russell threw up his hands.

"We all know you see her as a little sister, Nick. I didn't mean anything by it." Nick adjusted his hat as he tried to calm down.

"I'll be back in a few hours unless you're done. Feel free to use the office as your meeting spot once everyone's back. You and Betty have Lucy's number, so between her, me, and Dad, you'll be able to get in. And if you're going to be here for a bit... I'd consider giving you a spare."

"I'd appreciate that, Smith. You got a working coffee pot right?"

"Kitchen, right through there. Bathroom is across the hall from that. Help yourself to whatever food and drinks are there. You and Dad should order some pizzas."

"I'll get on that," Mason said, pulling out his phone. "You two head out. Thomas and I have this."

"Please call me-"

"I *will*." Nick nodded and walked out to the car. He got in and started backing out.

"Where to?" Jimmy asked.

"Outlet," Nick said. "We'll get something for Lucy and maybe something for the baby."

"Like what?"

"Well... When I learned your mom was pregnant, I got you a bear with an Army uniform. I didn't know how long I'd be working, and I didn't want you to forget about me."

"Don't I still have that somewhere?"

"You slept with it until you were eight," Nick said with a soft smile.

"So. You're not active Army anymore. What if we got a bear with like… a Sherlock Holmes hat and a long coat? That's a pretty 'detective-y' thing, right?"

"If we can find it."

"There's a toy shop in the outlets. We can try there." Nick nodded and headed that way.

INTERLUDE

Leesburg

He watched this… detective come out of his office. He'd just *left* his son alone. He was just like them. He didn't deserve his son.

He'd take him, too.

Then they'd be a family. All five children. His new children. He smirked and started his truck, carefully following the detective down the street.

CHAPTER 9

"You're *sure* Lucy will like this?" Jimmy looked at the book Nick was holding.

"Do you not know your own wife? She said that's her favorite childhood book. That *plus* the bear… Trust me, Dad. She'll love it."

"Hm. Alright. Let's go check out and then head to the toy store." Nick put a gentle hand on Jimmy's head and led him to the register.

"Is this it for you?" the cashier asked.

"Can I get a candy bar?"

"Hurry," Nick agreed. Jimmy grinned and put a bar of chocolate on the counter. Nick gave him an amused look as he handed the woman cash to purchase the book and candy. The cashier put the book in a plastic bag and handed the candy to Jimmy.

"Thanks! Thanks, Dad."

"Let's get to the toy store."

"Yes sir," Jimmy said as he put the candy in his back pocket for later. He walked with Nick down a row of stores to the brightly lit one. They stepped in and Nick grimaced.

"Your mom took care of most of this," he admitted. "I was gone for most of…"

"You were home for the important parts. Bears are over there. We're probably going to have to special order the hat, but I'm sure we can find the coat." Nick just nodded and allowed Jimmy to lead him to the stuffed animals.

"What about this one?" He asked, holding up a bear for Jimmy to see.

"No. It's too light."

"This one?"

"Too dark."

"Alright, Goldilocks. This one?"

"Just right," Jimmy smirked. Nick chuckled and they walked around the store, looking for clothes for the bear.

"I don't think we're going to find anything here for a *bear*."

"Here," Jimmy said, pulling out his phone. "I'll check online." He typed a few things into his phone. "How much are you willing to spend?"

"How much is it?" Nick asked, already knowing it would be expensive.

"It's $36 for a detective set."

"It's clothes for a *toy*. You've got to be kidding me."

"Is that really too much for my baby brother? And to get out of the doghouse with Lucy?" Nick raised his eye.

"You're so sure it's a boy?"

"Well, yeah. Grandpa only has boys, Uncle Robbie has a boy… It's not hard to believe you and Lucy will have a boy, too." Nick blinked.

"We'll be revisiting family life this year. I'll make the changes to your schedule when we get home."

"Great… So are you gonna get it?"

"Send me the link and then use my account to buy it," he told Jimmy as he handed him his phone. Jimmy did as Nick said while they walked to the register.

"Done," Jimmy said. Nick took his phone back and barely suppressed a sigh.

"How much after shipping?"

"Um."

"Jimmy."

"Closer to $50."

"Kid's already costing an arm and a leg," Nick muttered.

"Yeah, but think of how happy Lucy will be, especially once you tell her you did the same thing for me."

"We won't be able to give her the bear until after we get the outfit."

"It'll be in in less than a week," Jimmy shrugged.

"Great." Nick moved up in line and handed the cashier the bear.

"Is this it for you?"

"It is. Jim, you want to head on to the car?"

"Sure, Dad." Nick handed the keys to him and pulled out his wallet at the same time. Once he was sure Jimmy was gone, he put a single Army man he found on the counter.

"Wasn't going to steal it," he felt the need to say. "I just wanted to surprise my son. It's… it's an inside story." The cashier just gave him a fake smile as he rang it up. Nick paid, grabbed his bag, and walked out. He got to the car and frowned at it still being locked.

"Jimmy?" He called. "Jimmy, where are you?" He retraced his steps to the toy store and froze.

His keys were on the sidewalk with a bar of chocolate.

The chocolate he'd just bought Jimmy. Nick narrowed his eyes at the folded paper he saw under his keys. He pulled it out to read it.

Detective Smith,
You should have protected him.
He's mine now.
They're all mine. I will be their
father and they will be my children.
Don't come after my family or I will kill you.

Nick fell to his knees. It took all of his training to not completely collapse, and after a few breaths, he was able to pull out his phone.

The phone Jimmy had just used for him. Nick pressed a button with shaky hands.

"Johns."

"He has Jimmy."

"What? Nicky,"

"He was here and now he's gone."

"This isn't funny. What the hell are you talking about?"

"He took my son!" Nick couldn't stop the sob. Jimmy was his life- everyone knew that.

"Ok. Ok- call the police, Nick. Where are you?"

"Outlet."

"*I'll be there in a second. Thomas, I need you to drive me and we need the sirens.*" The phone slid out of Nick's hand as he stared at the candy bar. Jimmy hardly asked for anything from stores. It had been years since he requested *candy*.

He was only fourteen. He was still so young-Nick took a shuddered breath and grabbed his phone again. He called 911.

"*911, what's your emergency?*"

"My son. My son has been kidnapped."

"*Where are you? What's your name?*"

"I'm at the Outlet Mall in Leesburg. My name is Nicholas Smith. Please... please send Deputy Frintz."

"*I have units on the way, sir. Please stay on the line-*"

"I can't. I have to call my wife." Nick hung up and wiped a tear as he pressed the button for Lucy.

"*Nick, I'm still not-*"

"Jimmy's been taken."

"*Where are you?*"

"Outlet."

"*I'm on my way.*" Nick hung up and sniffed, quickly drying his face. He could break down later. Jimmy needed him *now*. He wiped his eyes, schooled his face, and stood up straight as he heard sirens approach him. He would not let them see how affected he was by this. He was *Sergeant Nicholas Smith*. He was a retired member of Special Forces.

"Nicky!" Mason ran over and pulled him into a hug. Just like that, Nick's resolve crumbled and he wept into his father's shoulder.

His son was gone.

CHAPTER 10

Jimmy groaned as he felt himself waking up with a massive headache. He tried opening his eyes, but found that it was a harder task than usual. When they finally opened to small slits, he was confused.

He remembered leaving the toy store to go to the car, and then *pain*. Now he was on a bed- a bed that *definitely* wasn't his- in a room he'd never seen before.

Jimmy took a breath. What would his dad do? He did a quick assessment of his injuries. A headache, a sore shoulder, and his left ankle felt weird. Jimmy lifted his hand and felt the back of his head from where most of the pain was coming. There was a crusty feeling. Dried blood. Jimmy swallowed.

"Are you awake?" He heard a young male whisper. Jimmy carefully turned his head towards the voice.

"I think so. Where am I?"

"I don't know. I've been here for a week. But I don't recognize you. I recognized the others from pictures online, but I don't know you. And he didn't hurt us bringing us in-"

"Are you Rob... Something?" Jimmy's head throbbed at the attempt to think.

"Yeah. Rob Whitten. How did you know?"

"My dad is looking for you." Dad. Jimmy knew Nick wouldn't stop looking for the missing kids, and now that *he* was with them… Jimmy just hoped Nick could figure out they were together. He sniffed and tried to hide his tears. He was afraid.

"It'll be ok. How old are you?"

"Just turned fourteen," Jimmy admitted, feeling embarrassed.

"Me too. You said your dad is looking for me? Are you from Chesapeake, too?"

"Leesburg."

"How does your dad know-?"

"Your parents came to him. He's a P.I."

"Huh. That's cool. What about the others?"

"Their parents came to him, too. Separately." Jimmy rubbed his temples.

"You ok?"

"My head… Everything hurts."

"Ok. Um… I can get King. He'll get you some medicine."

"Who?"

"The guy who took us."

"He… You know who he is?"

"Yeah." Jimmy paled. He'd always heard that if you knew your captor… getting out alive wasn't in the plans. "It'll be ok. He's… He went to school with my dad. He won't hurt us."

"Maybe not you," Jimmy said quietly as his head throbbed. He watched as Rob knocked on the door. A flap slid open.

"Yes?"

"We need medicine in here." Nothing. "We need medicine please, *Dad*."

"I'll bring some in a moment. Are you hurt, son?"

"No. The new… brother is."

"Oh. No, he's being punished."

"He could have a concussion. He can't learn the rules if he has a concussion." The flap slid closed.

"He makes you call him 'Dad?'"

"Yeah. He stopped giving me food until I did. It's…"

"You don't have to explain," Jimmy said. "He hasn't… *done* anything to you, has he?"

"King? No. No way. He just…" A cat flap at the bottom of the door lifted and a tray with some Tylenol and a glass of water was pushed in.

"Take this, son." Jimmy recoiled at the voice aimed towards him.

"I'm not your son!" Rob's eyes went wide and he pushed himself against the wall. All Jimmy could hear was a chuckle.

"You're mine now, Andrew."

"My na-" Jimmy stopped talking as Rob shook his head, eyes still wide. Instead he took the medicine before 'King' decided to take it back.

"He gave all of us new names," Rob said once they heard footsteps walking away from the door.

"You've seen the others?"

"Abby, Wendy, and Rahne. He calls them

Rachel, Mary, and Patricia."

"And you?"

"John." Jimmy felt a pang in his heart. Would Grandpa be looking for him, too?

"And you've just… *let* him?"

"I tried fighting. I got hungry. You get food if you're good."

"He can do whatever he wants. My name is my *name*. I'm not…"

"You'll be hungry enough eventually."

"My dad…"

"He can't help you here-"

"My dad was Special Forces. He used to tell me stories about what he went through. He once went over a week without food. I can do that, too." Rob just shook his head.

"You'll see." Jimmy carefully moved his water from the tray to under his bed. He knew he could go without food- his dad had talked about it enough- but water… Water was a necessity. Jimmy folded his arms over his already growling stomach. He was supposed to have eaten pizza with his dad, grandpa, and SSA Thomas.

"What time is it?"

"It's close to dinner." Almost as if Rob had been heard, a bell rang. Jimmy heard metal scraping and the doors opened.

"What's going on?"

"Dinner. Look- I know you want to be brave, but… Your dad would want you to survive, right?" Jimmy said nothing as he followed Rob out of the room, slightly limping. They met up with three girls, one older, and two who looked alike and were definitely younger, and walked into a large dining room. The four sat like they were used to everything already. Jimmy paled. The twins had only been missing for a few days, and they were already-

"Have a seat, Andrew."

"My name is Jimmy." Jimmy looked the man up and down. "You can call me Mr. Smith." 'King' smirked and leaned down so he was eye level with Jimmy.

"Your name is Andrew."

"My name is Jimmy. Go ahead. I'm prepared to starve. My dad-"

"*I* am your father now."

"My father is Nicholas Smith, a private investigator for the state of Virginia, consultant of the FBI. He-" Jimmy's head jerked to the side and he felt a strange heat on his cheek. His eyes watered on their own at the sting. His dad... He never slapped his face. He said that wasn't discipline. Jimmy took a shaky breath.

"What do you think now, *Andrew*?"

"I think you hit like a coward-" His face jerked to the side again. He could taste the coppery blood in his mouth. Jimmy took a breath. "Is that all you-?" Jimmy groaned and doubled over, arms protecting his abdomen from another blow.

"I think..." 'King' said. "You'll have dinner and then we'll have a private conversation later

about how you're supposed to talk to your father."
Jimmy paled as 'King' pushed him into a seat. He
wanted his dad.

Why wasn't Nick there yet?

CHAPTER 11

Jimmy cried into his pillow. His back hurt and the backs of his legs felt like they were on fire. His dad had threatened the belt on numerous occasions, but he'd never... It hurt. Jimmy had tried to stay brave and not make a sound, but he couldn't stay that way for long. 'King' kept whipping until blood was drawn. Jimmy only knew that because he saw the drops on the floor.

"Where are you, Dad?" he cried quietly. He took back everything he'd said about Lucy's cake. He'd eat the whole thing if it meant he had his family again.

"Are you... Are you ok?"

"I want my dad." Jimmy didn't care to act brave any more. Nick had told him over and over he was a child and was expected to act as such. Children could cry for their parents. Jimmy sniffed.

His dad didn't cry. Even when everyone thought Grandpa was going to die, Jimmy never saw him shed a tear. Jimmy knew he had to be like Nick to survive.

"We'll figure out a way to leave eventually," Rob said, trying to be comforting.

"He's going to kill me."

"No, no he said he just wants-"

"He wants a family with *you*. He said he took me because he heard my dad was looking for him. Him having me is supposed to stop my dad from continuing the search."

"Will he?"

"No." There was quiet, except for the sniffling from Jimmy.

"Is he really good at finding things?"

"He found a serial killer the FBI couldn't track down." Jimmy blinked back new tears as he thought of that night that now felt like ages ago, despite it being just over a year.

"You said he helped the FBI. Do you think he'll ask them for help?"

"He had already brought them in before... me. My grandpa's former partner was at my dad's office when he and I left to get-" Jimmy swallowed. Would he ever get to be a big brother? Had his dad told Lucy? Had his dad told *anyone*?

Did his dad even care? A new baby was coming... He knew his dad had always said one kid was all he wanted. Jimmy swallowed the lump in his throat.

"Will they- What did they know?"

"Your friends saw you get in a green truck. Same with the twins, I think. Dad didn't have as much time to go over that case with me."

"He talks to you about his cases?"

"Yeah. I help him with some of them every now and then."

"And you know FBI agents?"

"One was in my dad and stepmom's wedding. She's like an aunt to me. And SSA Thomas… he likes me. They won't stop until I'm found. And they're looking for you guys, too. And my grandpa was one of the best agents before an injury forced him to retire a year ago. Now he helps my dad. Dad sent him to your parents house on Friday."

"Really?"

"Your sister Julie misses you."

"I never thought I'd miss that pain." Jimmy heard sniffing and knew it wasn't him this time.

"I just found out I was going to be a brother. Now I don't know-" Jimmy blinked back tears. The lights in the room turned off.

"We should sleep. He does checks…" Jimmy dried his face and pulled the blanket over him. He hissed as the weight of the blanket pressed on his back.

He had to be brave. His dad would be brave. Jimmy closed his eyes and drifted to sleep, dreaming of his dad taking him fishing again.

CHAPTER 12

Nick sat at his desk, numb. People were talking to him, but he couldn't *hear* them. All he could think about was his son... Missing. Afraid. Alone.

"Nick?" Nick looked at the exhausted form of his wife. The delivery had been hard on her and the twins... Only one baby had made it. "This is your son." Nick picked up the squirming bundle from the hospital's bassinet into his arms, body tensed and afraid- not that he'd admit it. He heard Carol laughing and he looked at her with wide eyes.

"Am I doing it wrong?"

"Hold him to you." She carefully sat up, groaning as gravity pulled her sensitive stomach and stitches down. Once her breath was even, she corrected Nick's arms, helping him hold their son against his chest. Nick looked at the baby and felt a smile forming.

"Hi Jimmy. I'm your daddy."

Nick felt a hand on his shoulder and jumped. The face came into focus. Mason. Nick blinked, trying to understand what he was saying.

"...shock. He can't..."

So he was in shock. That made sense. The Army prepared him for a lot of things: hunger, pain, thirst, losing friends, losing *limbs*, dying... It didn't prepare him for his son being taken from him while he was just a few feet away.

"... security cameras. A white man in a green truck..."

It *was* the guy. The note said it was, but having more proof-

"... used something to hit his head. He didn't have a chance..."

He hurt his son? Nick narrowed his eyes. The other kids were taken peacefully-

"He's going to kill him," Nick heard himself whisper. He felt a calloused hand turning his face. Mason again.

"We're going to get this guy, Nick. I swear."

"He said-"

"And *you've* had your life threatened by a madman before. Jimmy-"

"That was my life. Jimmy is my son. He shouldn't be in that position. It should have been me that was taken- You don't understand-" A firm hand gripped his upper arm.

"I think I know what a father is willing to do for his son, Nicky." Nick's eyes moved to Mason's chest where he knew the scar was from Anderson. "We can't... Jimmy is probably waiting for us to spring him, kid. We can't let him down. Now are you ok enough to talk with the cops and Russ? You know how important the first few hours-" Mason stopped and Nick saw him tear up.

"I'm ready." He looked up and saw several deputies and the FBI team waiting for him.

When had they gotten back? Betty was comforting Lucy. Nick appreciated that. He couldn't... He couldn't be strong for her right now. He was glad someone could.

"What were you doing at the Outlet?" Nick looked and saw Deputy Frintz. At least she knew Jimmy wouldn't have run away like the others had assumed of the missing kids. One of the benefits of Jimmy growing up in a small town like Leesburg. Everyone knew almost everyone.

"We," Nick cleared his throat. "We were getting a gift for Lucy and the baby."

"What baby?" She asked, writing things down.

"Lucy's pregnant. Jimmy and I were getting a teddy bear- I'd gotten him one when his mom told me she was pregnant."

"Anything else?"

"I bought him that candy bar."

"What candy bar?"

"The one by my keys and the note. He never asks for things, definitely not candy..."

"Why was he separated from you?" Frintz asked.

"He- I asked him to start the car. I was buying him an Army man..." Nick swallowed. "Just a silly reminder that I was still there for him. I didn't want him to see it so sent him ahead. I left and went to the car. I couldn't find him, so I went back towards the toy store. I saw my keys. I read the note. I called my dad."

"And this note. Do you understand what it means?"

"You don't?"

"If it's a case you're working on," Deputy Frintz said, "then no."

"Kidnappings all over Virginia. Louisa, Chesapeake, Charlottesville. Now Leesburg. He knew I was looking for him and he took my son." Nick didn't stop the quiet tears from falling. His kid was missing. Who would judge-?

"So the big bad Nick Smith can be reduced to a quivering mess after all." Nick didn't realize he'd moved until he saw Agent Green against the wall with his hands holding her there, tightening around her neck.

"My *son* is missing because I was doing the job police officers refused to do, you bitch. His life is being threatened if I-" Nick didn't stop Mason from pulling him away from her, standing between them.

"We're going to find him, Nicky."

"He's alone, Dad. He's alone and scared and waiting for me, and-"

"He's a Johns, no matter what his name is. He might be scared, but he's not going to give up, Nick. I didn't give up in Russia. You didn't give up in foster care-"

"It's not the same. He was *taken*-" Mason shook his head.

"Breathe, Nick." Nick took a breath and slowly let it out. "I know your son is missing.

Everyone is here to help find him and the others, and they're here for *you*, too. You're not alone. We all love Jimmy and we're going to get him back. But I need you to *stop thinking about him-*"

"How can you-?!" Mason grabbed Nick's shoulders and shook him. The shock of being roughly handled by his father caused Nick's eyes to shoot open. He didn't know if he should be angry, terrified, or relieved that at least *someone* was able to take control in this situation.

"Don't see him as your son, Nick! Turn off the emotion and look at this objectively. He's a missing child. What would you tell the parents?"

"I… I don't-"

"Yes you do!" Mason said as he shook him again. Nick blinked and took a breath before nodding to Mason.

"The note. He- he only left a note for me, not the other parents. He said he- they would be a family. That means he doesn't plan on hurting the others."

"And that's *good.*"

"It means… They're missing, but they're *safe*. We won't go looking and find b-bodies," he said, voice hitching at the thought of his son, lifeless. Mason let Nick's shoulders go.

"There's my boy. Alright. All of the parents who were at the reunion have been warned. What *next*?"

"Amber Alerts. Even if the others don't… He- I have *proof* Jimmy was taken. FBI should put out an Amber Alert for all five of them, but definitely Jimmy." Mason nodded and looked up.

"Russ. Have you put out an alert, yet?"

"On it, Boss." Mason gave him a look and Russ just gave him a sheepish smile. "Habit." Within seconds, everyone in the room had their phones shrieking with the alert. Nick took his phone out to silence it.

Abducted Child- James Smith, 14, Leesburg, Virginia- Nick handed his phone to Mason to exit out of it and took a shuddered breath.

"We should get it on the news. The video- at least the *truck*. Someone had to have seen the truck, right?" Mason nodded to Jeremy.

"Nicky, he's a minor. We need permission to blast his picture *everywhere*." Nick nodded once. "Betty-"

"You need to stop delegating," Agent Green said. "You're not one of us-"

"Agent Green," Russell snapped. "We are here to *help*. Mason Johns has been doing this longer than you've been alive, so shut. Up." Nick didn't even have the energy to smirk.

"Betty, can you take Lucy home and find a recent picture of him to put on the news?"

"I need to stay-"

"I'll bring you right back, Lucy," Betty said quietly. "Jimmy needs you to do this. Nick needs you. I don't think he'll be able to manage this right now." Lucy nodded and allowed Betty to walk her out. Mason led Nick back to his desk.

"I can't-"

"If someone calls, Nick," Mason gently told him. Nick sat and pulled his office phone to him.

"Dad?"

"Yeah?"

"Jimmy… I have a phone locator. Can Russ or Jeremy…?"

"I'll start doing that now," Jeremy said, pulling his laptop out.

"Smith." Nick looked up and saw Deputy Frintz. "We're going to find him. I've watched him grow up. If there's anyone who can make it back…"

"Thank you."

"I'm going to go and get some others to start helping me patrol. I doubt he's here, but we can go ask around."

"Thank you," Mason told her.

"We might not all… Care for Smith and his tactics, but we love Jimmy." Deputy Frintz left the office and Nick closed his eyes, hoping to wake up from the nightmare. The quiet murmurs were interrupted by pounding on the door. Agent Green straightened her blazer and opened it.

"He's closed-" But the person just pushed her aside.

"Nicky!" Nick opened his eyes.

"Robbie? What-?"

"Dad called us. Kaya dropped me off and is meeting Lucy at the house. What can I do?"

CHAPTER 13

Not a single call during the night. Not that Nick thought there would be. Hoped, of course. But realistically... Most people saw the alerts and ignored them. He was certainly guilty of it.

"You need to get some sleep-"

"How can I?" He asked his younger brother. "Someone could call at any minute."

"You look like shit, Nick. Jimmy needs you at 100%. Can you honestly say you're in any condition to-?" Nick turned his body. Robbie sighed and looked at Mason, who looked just as tired as Nick.

"Just another few minutes," Mason said. "I'll take him home kicking and screaming if I need to." There was a brief knock on the door.

"Hello? Nick?" Nick turned and looked at the door.

"Karen?"

"We got an alert last night. Is it really...?" Nick nodded. "Ok. We're here to help." She stepped back out and then returned seconds later with several people from town carrying bags of steaming food, boxes of coffee, donuts, biscuits... Nick stopped looking at the food and eyed the woman who had been his bartender and friend for several years.

"Why?"

"As often as you've helped us?"

"Thank you."

"What can we do?" Robbie stepped forward before Nick could decline their help.

"Can you help man the phones for tips? Nick and our dad have been up all night."

"Got it." Karen turned to Nick. "Go home. Sleep. We'll take care of this and if something comes in, you'll know immediately."

"I can't-"

"Nick," Mason said. "These people are here to help. Let them help. We both need sleep. Robbie's right- Jimmy needs you and you're no good to him like this. And I'm not good to *you* like this."

"You can't make me leave." Mason stepped closer to Nick, invading his personal space.

"I will throw you over my shoulder and carry you out if I have to. You're going *home*, Nick. At least four hours." Nick saw the determination on Mason's face and turned his head.

"Ok," he relented. He had no desire to test Mason's threat, and he was too tired to fight.

"Good." Mason put a hand on Nick's back and gently pushed him out the door and to his car.

"Where's Lucy?" Nick asked as they climbed in the car.

"She went home to sleep last night. You don't remember?" Nick shook his head. "We're going to find him, Nick."

"Alive?" Nick asked with a thick voice.

"Yes." Mason started the car, but turned to look at his son before driving off. "I gave up, Nick. I gave up and you were abused. I gave up and Robbie was told he was only there because their birth son died and he was a *replacement*. You're like me in enough ways. Don't be like me in that way, son." Nick put his head on the window and let out a slow breath. Mason shook his head and drove away.

"I'm sorry."

"For what?"

"This is my fault. If I hadn't let him go to the car alone-"

"He'd have gotten him at a different time. I read the note. He was prepared for this." Mason parked on the street in front of Nick's house. "Go. Bed." Nick gave his father an incredulous look. Mason was sending him to *bed* like a child?

"You can't send me-"

"Go, Nicky." Nick opened the door and got out.

"Four hours?"

"Four hours," Mason agreed. Nick closed the door and walked up to the house. He stepped in and saw Lucy sitting on the couch with her phone in her hands. She looked up, confused.

"Nick?"

"Karen, Fran, Rick... Everyone I've helped came to the office this morning. They brought breakfast and..."

"And what?"

"They're waiting for calls to come in." Lucy

nodded.

"Ok. Let's get you out of those clothes and into bed. You need to sleep-"

"Mason said he'd be here in four hours."

"Then sleep, babe. If a call comes in, you know they'll tell you." Nick nodded and went to their room. He stripped and put on a pair of pajama pants, in case someone came to the house, and got into bed.

"Daddy? Where's Mommy?" Nick crouched down and put his hands on Jimmy's small arms.

"Mommy died, Jimmy. A man… A man broke the law and because of that, she died."

"When is she coming back?" Nick just pulled Jimmy into a hug.

"She's not, baby. It's just us now."

"Is it because I was bad?" Nick gently pushed Jimmy back out and looked in his eyes.

"Absolutely not, Jimmy. Mommy loves-" Nick stopped and looked over Jimmy's head for a minute before meeting his eye again. "Your actions didn't do this. Neither did mine. And Mommy was being as safe as she could, but because someone else broke the law, she's gone."

"Oh."

"We're going to be ok, Jimmy. Daddy will always be here to protect you."

"I know, Daddy."

Nick blinked back tears. He'd promised Carol that nothing would happen to their son. He promised *Jimmy* nothing would happen to him.

He'd failed them both.

Nick sat up and left his room, going into Jimmy's. He found the Army bear on a shelf and took it down, hugging it to him. He lied on Jimmy's bed, smelling Jimmy's shampoo on the pillow. He finally fell asleep, dreaming of holding his son again.

INTERLUDE

They had to move. He'd gotten the alert last night- who *hadn't*? The women at the store this morning kept giving him odd looks. The man stared at his car a little too long.

It wasn't safe.

"Children? We're going to go on a family vacation. No, let's not wear your nice picture clothes. Go put on something else that will be comfortable walking in. Rachel, darling, please help your sisters dress. Andrew, John. You both change as well."

"It's Jimmy." He grabbed Andrew's arm and yanked him forward, taking pleasure in the snap he'd felt after all of the problems the boy was giving him.

"*Andrew* will rejoin you in a moment, John. Go do as I have requested." He let Andrew go and began unbuckling his belt, satisfied at the fear he saw on Andrew's face.

CHAPTER 14

Mason sat up in bed and rubbed his face. Four hours of sleep after a sleepless night wasn't enough, but while Jimmy was missing… It was too much. Mason got out of bed and rushed to put on fresh clothes and his hat, knowing Nick was likely pacing the floor as he waited. He grabbed his phone, keys, and wallet and ran to his car, tucking his shirt in as he went. Mason sped as fast as he dared to Nick's house and nearly skidded to a park on the street. He cut the engine and went up the sidewalk, knocking on the door.

"He's still asleep," Lucy said through the door.

"Good. Were there any…?" Mason asked as he entered the house.

"I would have woken him up if there were. Can I get you anything?"

"Can I get *you* anything? You look about dead on your feet, Lucy."

"I just want my son back."

"We've got the best people on it. He'll be home soon." Lucy gave a jerky nod. "I need to wake him up. If he sleeps much longer, he'll be back to Pissy Nick." That got Lucy smiling, which was Mason's intention.

"He's in Jimmy's room." Mason took Lucy's

hand.

"We're going to bring him home. That's the son of Nick Smith- kid's probably figured out how to escape now and is biding his time to get the others out with him."

"That does sound like something Nick would do."

"Exactly. Now do you want to wake him up, or do you want me to?"

"I should. I don't think he'd appreciate anyone else seeing how vulnerable he is right now." Lucy gave Mason a small smile and went down the hall. He heard quiet voices. Mason looked around the room, trying to figure out what was *off*... There were a few pictures up of Nick and Lucy's wedding, a copy of the Johns family before he was a POW and Jenny was murdered, one of Jimmy and his mother, Carol, and the rest... were gone. Mason frowned for a moment before he saw all of the frames on the dining room table. Clearly Lucy and Betty had spent quite some time picking just the perfect picture of Jimmy to share.

"I'll be ready in a second, Dad. Sorry." Mason said nothing as he heard a door close. Lucy returned to the main room, tears coursing down her cheeks.

"Are- what happened?"

"He was curled up with Jimmy's bear. He's not handling this well, Mason."

"No, I'd imagine he wasn't. Once Jimmy's back, everything will get back to normal. He'll be overprotective for… a while, but it'll get better."

"I hope so. I'm worried about him- about both of them."

"Ready?" Nick asked as he came down the hall, putting his hat on straight.

"Yeah. Let's go."

"Are you coming too, Luce?"

"Do you… Do you want me there?"

"You're my wife, and you're Jimmy's mother. You've been in his life longer than Carol…" Nick blinked at the realization that his current wife had been a mother figure to his son longer than the boy's biological mother…

"Just let me get my shoes on." Mason and Nick waited for her to slide them on before heading back to the car.

"Any news?" Nick asked, both hoping for something and dreading what might be said.

"None that's been shared with me." Nick had Lucy sit in the front seat as he climbed into the back of the car. Mason, taking Lucy's pregnancy into account, drove the speed limit to Nick's office.

When they arrived, it was a flurry of activity. Mason frowned as he saw Russell in the front sending people to their cars. He pulled up and rolled down the window.

"What's going on?"

"There you are! You weren't answering your phone, Mase. There's been a confirmed sighting of the truck and the guy by different people."

"Where?"

"Loudoun. We're getting teams there now. People here are asking to help search, but I don't know what to expect while there."

"Where's Robbie?"

"Inside, still trying to call you." Mason put the car in park and jumped out to go in the office.

"Robbie! Let's go!"

"I'll meet you there," Mason heard Kaya say. "Go be with Nick." Robbie came into view.

"Did Russ-?"

"Loudoun. I've got Nick and Lucy in the car now."

"Where's your phone?" Mason pulled it out of his pocket. He tried checking his voicemail but only got a black screen.

"Dead, apparently."

"Charge it on the way. Let's go." They got into Mason's car and Mason waited for Russell to pull out. He followed him, grateful for Betty getting behind him, sirens on.

"Loudoun?" Nick asked.

"Yeah. I've never heard of it."

"It's close," Nick said. He opened the GPS on his phone and typed in the city. "See- fifteen minutes away. Have the other parents been informed?"

"I don't know."

"Let me call Betty." Lucy put her phone to her ear and waited. "Betty, Nick wants to know if the other parents have been informed." Lucy turned to look at her husband. "She said not yet."

"Ask if it's alright that I do it."

"He wants to know if he can, since it was his case to begin with." Lucy nodded and Nick went through his contacts list, dialing Frances Hannen's number first and put the call on speakerphone..

"Hello?"

"Mrs. Hannen, this is Nick Smith-"

"Mr. Smith! I heard about your son. Are you ok?"

"No. But we have a lead from the Amber Alert. He was spotted in Loudoun, Virginia. We're on our way with the FBI right now."

"Are we allowed to be there as well?"

"Ma'am, I'm not a federal agent, so I can't tell you one way or another. I just know this poor excuse of a man has taken my son and there's no one who can tell me to stay away."

"I'm on my way." Nick hung up and dialed Richard Whitten's number next, again on speakerphone.

"Whitten Residence."

"Mr. Whitten, this is Nick Smith-"

"I'm not paying you until my son is home."

"And I wouldn't either. An Amber Alert was sent out last night for another child because it was day of-"

"Ah. Yes, we got that alert. I didn't realize it was for the same... It wasn't a name I recognized."

"That's because it was my son he took. Now we've gotten a tip from the alert. The truck and the man seen in the video taking my son were both spotted in Loudoun, Virginia. I'm on my way with the FBI right now."

"*And we're being told to stay while you-*"

"I'm not the one who makes these decisions, Mr. Whitten. But it's not illegal to take trips, and I'll be damned if I'm told to stay back while my son is here."

"*Thank you, Mr. Smith. We'll be there as soon as we can.*" Nick hung up and rubbed his face.

"Why does he have to be such a dick?" he muttered as he called the Fredericks' number.

"*Hello?*"

"Mr. Fredericks?"

"*Speaking.*"

"This is Nick Smith. We have a few witnesses who saw the green truck and the man who's responsible for the kidnappings this morning in Loudoun, Virginia. We're on our way with the FBI right now."

"*Can we-?*"

"I don't have that authority, Mr. Fredericks. I just know... He took my son because of my involvement, and I'm not letting the Feds stop me. In fact, I'm in a car between two of *theirs* and I plan to stay that way until we get there."

"*We're coming, too.*" Nick hung up and put his phone beside him.

"You know they're going to be pissed, right?"

"I don't... Dad, I don't *care*. Would you have let them keep you away from us?"

"Not for a second."

"And I *don't* have the authority to tell them to stay away. I'm just a P.I. And Betty *knew* that, or else I wouldn't have been given the green light to call."

"I'm sure *Agent Green* will have a thing or two to say about this."

"She can choke on a dick."

"Nick!" Mason saw Lucy blushing and he stifled a laugh.

"Like her or not, she's a federal agent-"

"And that immediately demands respect? No. She came into *my* city and acted like she owned it. I'm not putting up with that. This was my case. It'd *still* be my case if-" Nick stopped and Mason saw him struggling to get the words out.

"I know, Nick. I'm pretty sure Russ wanted to keep his head on his neck or we wouldn't be on our way." Mason looked in the rear view mirror and saw Robbie with his hand on Nick's shoulder. The look he had was of obvious concern for his brother, yet relief that it wasn't his own son.

"How long will we be there?" Robbie asked.

"I don't know. A few hours. A few days. A week."

"Should I have Kaya bring us some clothes? I can't see us leaving the city..."

"That would... Yeah, kid. That'd be great." Mason hadn't even thought of clothes.

"Can-?" Nick closed his mouth.

"What Nick?"

"Can you ask her to bring some clothes for Jimmy?"

"Yeah. Not a problem." Robbie got out his phone and started typing a message to his wife.

"So. I haven't heard from you for a while."

"It's August."

"And?"

"Classes have started. I had seven different syllabi due in July- four that had to be done from scratch because they loaded me down with classes this semester. Classes started two weeks ago. I've been at the school or asleep. My own kid has barely seen me."

"But you're here-?"

"My family needed me."

CHAPTER 15

"Come on, kids! We've got to move!" Jimmy blinked back tears as his arm moved. He'd never felt so much pain in his life. He got in line with the other children and they left the cabin. 'King' had them walk a ways from the cabin and Jimmy saw the green truck. He took a shuddered breath.

His dad would find him- them. He hadn't given up. But if they kept moving, it would be harder.

"Abby," he whispered to the girl beside him.

"What?"

"How fast are you?"

"I run track. I'm fast."

"Can you-?"

"He'll catch me. I can't..."

"If I cause a distraction, you can. The question is *will* you?"

"Why?"

"Because if we get too far... My dad's looking for us. I know he is. We can be found if we stay *close*."

"How do you know he's looking? Rob and I have been here for over a week. Our parents haven't rescued us."

"This is what my dad does for a living. He was trained by the Army-"

"My uncle is in the Army. He doesn't do this stuff."

"My dad was a Green Beret."

"I don't know what that means."

"Do you know what a Navy SEAL is?"

"Um… Didn't Vin Diesel play one in a movie?" Jimmy blinked.

"Yeah, yeah I think so."

"Ok, then I've heard of them. His arms were *huge*-"

"Ok- that's the *Navy* version of my dad. He was the Army version."

"Ok. You're sure he's looking?"

"He'd do anything for me."

"What distraction are you going to make?"

"Give me a minute. When he comes near me, go to the kids and act like you're going to comfort them, and then *run*. Run towards the cabin and go the other direction from where we're going. My dad- Nick Smith. He'll be in a blue Tar Heels hat. My grandpa will probably be near him- Mason Johns. Also a Tar Heels hat." Jimmy swallowed. "My dad…"

"I'll tell him." Jimmy nodded.

"Get ready." Jimmy took a breath and braced himself for a new world of pain as he forced himself to fall forward.

"Ah! Dad! OW!" Abby moved to the younger girls and Rob, quickly whispering as 'King' had them stop to check on Jimmy.

"Andrew, what happened?"

"I tripped! Ah! It hurts!" Jimmy wasn't lying. His arm... He nearly passed out from the pain. He looked up and saw Abby quietly moving away before taking off in a sprint, unnoticed by their abductor. 'King' gave him a few minutes before forcing him up, causing a new wave of pain. Jimmy had to blink away the black spots slowly crowding his vision.

"We have to get moving. John! Help your brother. Show him where the roots are so he won't fall again." Rob walked over, gave Jimmy a nod and put his arm around him.

"She get away?" Jimmy asked in a hushed, pain-filled voice.

"Yeah." Jimmy whimpered as he adjusted his arm.

"Give me five minutes and then you do it, too. My grandpa said you were the star running back for your team?"

"Yeah. I can do it."

"I can't ask the twins..."

"I know. I'll find Abby and we'll find your dad and tell him everything."

"Be ready to run. Same thing- move like you're comforting the twins and then *go*. Go towards the cabin and then the opposite direction we're walking."

"Ok. What does your dad look like?"

"Like me. Tall. Muscles-almost like a white version of The Rock. Tattoo on his right arm with arrows and a knife in a shield- like shape with

Latin… Tar Heels hat."

"Ok. Got it."

"Ready?"

"Ready." Jimmy took a breath to brace himself before he intentionally fell again.

"Shit! Ow! Dad I can't walk!" Rob took a step back and moved to the twins as 'King' walked to Jimmy again.

"*Now* what, Andrew?!"

"I think I twisted my ankle my last fall! It hurts! I need- you need to carry me!" Jimmy knew it would slow him down considerably if he did that. Unless he left him. Rob swiftly moved to the side and was gone.

"I can't carry you!"

"A dad protects his children!" Jimmy cried. The man groaned and bent to pick Jimmy up. Jimmy was both relieved his plan worked and sickened that he was in the arms of the monster.

"John, keep the girls safe," 'King' said as he again led the way with Jimmy in his arms. After a silent ten minutes- or so Jimmy thought, since it was hard to keep track of the time, he heard the girls speaking quietly. He looked over 'King's' shoulder and caught their eyes, subtly shaking his head.

"Dad?"

"Yes, Patricia?"

"I'm Mary."

"*Yes*, Mary?" Jimmy bit his lips to stop the smirk. He liked these girls.

"Can we stop? I need to use the bathroom, and I'm sure Andrew does as well."

"And I'm hungry. You rushed us out before we finished lunch."

"We need to get further-"

"But I'm hungry!"

"I have to pee!"

"My feet hurt!"

"Mine too!" Jimmy could feel the man tense.

"Fine, just be quiet!" 'King' stopped and put Jimmy down on a tree stump. "John, watch your brother." 'King' looked around. "John? JOHN!"

"John!" The twins called together.

"John! Where are you?!" Jimmy said, following their lead. 'King' spun around.

"Rachel? Rachel?! RACHEL!" 'King' turned to Jimmy. "What did you do?!"

"I didn't do anything! I'm a *kid* with a broken arm and, and a screwed up ankle! And you've been *carrying* me! What could I have done?!"

"Don't you backtalk-" 'King' said as he slapped Jimmy across the face. Jimmy felt the white, burning pain and promptly threw up... Right on 'King's' shoes.

"I don't feel good," Jimmy groaned miserably.

"For the love of-"

"Dads are patient with sick kids. I need ginger ale to calm my stomach, remember?"

"I can't leave you here-"

"We'll keep Andrew safe. He can't walk. He

can't protect himself." Jimmy cringed at the idea of needing two little girls to 'protect' him, but he knew if he argued, 'King' would stay.

"I can't go anywhere. We'll stay here," he agreed.

"You need to hurry, Dad. We're in the woods and we don't know where we are, and it won't be long before it's dark."

"You three will stay here or *else*." Jimmy held his arm to him. He couldn't let him hurt Wendy or Rahne.

"We'll stay," Jimmy said again. 'King' nodded and walked away.

CHAPTER 16

Nick's jaw was locked. He refused to show any sign of anger or frustration as Russell continued to unleash his ire.

"You had no right to have them come here, Smith!"

"Russ-" Mason tried.

"I can't believe you said nothing to him! You know our protocols better than me and you let him-"

"I *did* say something. But you *know* him, Thomas. He's going to do what he wants, damn the consequences. Plus the hurt-"

"I know he's hurting right now, but he could have screwed everything up! These families are here- what if we have nothing for them?! What if what we have for them are dead and mangled bodies?!"

"They knew they weren't supposed to come-" Nick said, fists clenched.

"But you just *had* to tell them you were with us!"

"I could not *legally* tell them to stay away. If *you* had called-"

"They didn't need to know until we had *proof*!"

"Do you see the woods around here? We

need all the help we can get!" Nick cried.

"And when we find out he's gone?!"

"His truck won't have enough seats for *five teenagers*, especially if any of them are as tall as my son! And he won't let them ride in the bed of the truck because they would be seen. If he was here, he's traveling on foot. The safest place to do so is *in the woods*."

"If you're wrong and we've wasted time-" Mason stepped between his former second in command and his son.

"You forget it's because of *his son* that we got this far, Thomas. Why would he waste time?"

"The only reason you're here is because I value the time I spent working under you, Johns. But you are a civilian now and this is *my case*. You will remember that and you will keep him in line, or you're *both* out." Mason put a hand behind him to stop Nick from making it worse.

"We'll behave," he glared. Russell nodded and walked away.

"Thanks," Betty whispered.

"For what?" Nick asked.

"For not throwing me under the bus."

"Jimmy... He calls you his aunt, you know. If you got fired or transferred, he wouldn't be able to see you anymore. My son... I'd do anything to make him happy, Betty."

"I see him as a nephew, and nothing means more to me than my family. We're going to get him back, and we're going to get the guy who did this,

Nick. I promise." Nick nodded and allowed Mason to walk him over to where Russell was assigning groups to search parties.

"Smith! You're with Agent Lang. You too, Mason."

"What about me?" Robbie asked. Russell looked at him for a minute.

"You as well, then, Dr. Alderidge. Mr. and Mrs. Fredericks, you're with Agent Wilson. Mr. Whitten, you and your family are with Agent Green. Mrs. Hannen, you'll be with SSA Martin. I'll remain here unless someone finds... something. Keep me updated. Each group will have a radio for quick responses. Any questions?" Nick looked at the agent he was with. He looked like a child. Wild black hair, a sloppily buttoned shirt, blowing bubbles with his gum- *this* was the man he was supposed to 'listen' to?

"Dad," he said quietly. "Is there *any* way we can be put with a different agent?"

"Sorry, Smith," he heard Russell say. "I'm not going in and Betty and Jeremy will let you run roughshod over their orders. You don't like Agent Green, so that leaves Agent Lang. Unless you'd rather sit out?"

"You know damn well I'm going to look for my kid, *Agent Thomas.*"

"Then give him a chance. He's a good agent." Russell walked away and Agent Lang walked over.

"Hi. I'm Georgie- I mean Agent Lang. Sorry. Still getting used to that. You three ready?"

"Dear God, shoot me now," Nick muttered, rubbing his face. "Look, Agent Lang. My kid's out there-"

"Yeah, I know. Don't worry, Mr. Smith. I took a few courses that focused on kidnapping cases-some from Dr. Alderidge, in fact. We'll do what we can." Nick watched as the agent turned, took his group's radio, and started heading into the forest with their assigned search area.

"You had him in your class?" Nick asked his brother, completely bewildered.

"Maybe? I don't remember most of my students."

"You remembered Betty."

"Betty kept in touch. Do you remember each and every case you work on?"

"Not off the top of my head."

"Then why do you expect me to know this guy?"

"You're the college educated one-"

"And you're the life experience one-"

"Would you two *please stop*?" Mason said, sounding annoyed. "Dear lord, you're worse than when you were *kids*!"

"Sorry, Dad," the two said at the same time. Agent Lang looked back at the three, chuckling. Nick narrowed his eyes at him and Agent Lang quickly faced forward again.

"So, Agent Lang. How long have you been part of SSA Thomas' team?" Mason asked, trying to get to know the young agent.

"Oh, uh, three weeks? This is my first *real* assignment, so I hope it turns out well." Nick raised his fist, glaring at Mason as he forced it back down with a sharp look.

"I remember my first case-"

"That's right! You were an agent, too!"

"Helped train Russ," Mason said with a smile. "He was on my team the longest out of everyone else."

"I didn't realize you were... *him*."

"What do you mean by that?"

"These two are your sons, right? I guess I just didn't think you were *that* SSA Mason Johns after hearing their names." Nick stopped walking and took a breath.

"You think we can concentrate on finding these missing kids? Or is this going to be a question and answer session about Mason's time with the FBI? If so, I'll gladly separate-"

"You'll stay with the group, Nicholas," Mason warned. Robbie smirked at the indignant look on Nick's face.

"Our section starts about right here," Lang said after looking at his map. "Thomas, we're in our section," he spoke into the radio.

"Where did this guy come from?" Nick whispered to Robbie. "We're never going to find the kids with him. We can do this faster and more efficiently on our own." Nick felt a hand on his shoulder.

"If you separate, you'll be thrown off the

case and be forced to stay in the hotel room."

"You can't-"

"I'll cuff you to a chair myself," Mason threatened. "Like it or not, this is the agent we're working with. He might be inexperienced, but everyone has to start *somewhere*."

"That *somewhere* shouldn't be looking for *my son*."

"Just give him a chance, kid. He might surprise you." Mason patted Nick's shoulder and walked up to join Agent Lang.

"Is this how he's been since the doctor gave him the ok?"

"You just don't even *know*," Nick complained. "It's like he's a whole different person than from Mom's..." Nick rubbed his eyes. "He has grumpy old man syndrome." Robbie chuckled and took a look around. Trees were everywhere- which made sense, considering they were in a forest. Robbie sighed.

"What?"

"Just wondering how much help I'm going to be. Theoretically, I've got this. But... It's *Jimmy*."

"Tell me about it," Nick said as he scanned the area. "I feel like everything Special Forces taught me just... I can't think of any of it. And you're here, Robbie. That's more help than you realize. At least my family is here when I-"

"Hey, you see that?"

"See what?"

"Smoke." Nick followed his brother's line of

sight and his breathing became quicker.

"Dad?"

"*What*, Nick?"

"Robbie and I see smoke." Mason looked in the direction they were looking and then turned to Lang.

"Call it in to Thomas. It might be nothing, but we need to check it out." Lang nodded and informed Russell over the radio. The group followed the wisp in the air until they arrived at a cabin.

"A remote house," Nick said, trying to stop shaking. Mason knocked on the door and they waited for an answer.

Nothing.

Nick looked in the windows, trying to find *something* that would give them the right to enter.

"Anything?"

"Nothing. Looks like the smoke is from a fireplace that was recently put out, but I can't see… Wait." Nick cupped his hands over his eyes and looked intensely at the shirt he saw on the floor.

"What is it, Nicky?" Robbie asked, peering in with him.

"That's Jimmy's."

"You can't know that-" Agent Lang tried.

"No, that's his shirt. It was *mine*- he liked wearing it so I just gave it to him a few months ago. It has Sergeant Smith embroidered on it by my late wife, Jimmy's mom. I *know* that shirt. That's probable cause, right?" Agent Lang scratched his head.

"I… I don't know." Nick pushed past him and went to the door, first trying the doorknob.

"It's locked."

"We'll have to bust the door-" Nick was already on it. He tapped on the door, took a few steps back, and then kicked it open.

"I didn't think people could actually do that in one go," Robbie commented.

"Special Forces," Nick reminded him, grateful that while his thoughts were too scattered to think of the training, the physical aspect was still there.

"You were Special Forces?" Lang asked. "Did you know-?"

"Not important right now," Nick growled. "My kid's been here." He went in and flicked on the lights before he started exploring.

"SSA Thomas will be here in just a minute." Nick didn't acknowledge Lang as he looked around.

"There are *metal bars* on the doors," he noted angrily. He unlocked the first door and threw it open. He saw a feminine room with a set of bunk beds on one side and a twin sized bed on the other, both pressed against the walls.

"Dear God." Nick turned and saw Robbie and Mason looking into another room. He went to look in and saw a room for boys with two beds pushed against opposite walls.

One bed had signs of bloodstains.

"No," Nick said, feeling frozen.

"We don't know it was Jimmy, Nick." Nick watched Robbie walk in and examine the beds.

"Dad?" Mason went to Robbie and looked where he was pointing.

"Nick."

"What is it?"

"I need you to wait outside."

"No," he said, shaking his head. "You said it wasn't Jimmy!"

"I need you to wait outside," Mason repeated patiently. Nick stumbled backwards into a wall.

"I got him." Agent Lang helped lead Nick out. He walked with him, not daring to touch the man, through the house. They saw a dining room table with six chairs around it- five missing children and a deranged man, Nick realized. As they walked by, he saw a piece of paper and a *lot* of ink sitting innocently on the table.

"Wait!" Nick pulled away and grabbed the picture printed out on regular printer paper. He held it up to the light to see it better, and instead of tearing up like he thought he would, he felt himself get *angry* as he stormed out of the cabin, dropping the picture.

"What happened?" Robbie asked, coming out of the room looking pale.

"I don't know. He had this and-" Mason picked the picture up.

"Oh shit."

"What is it?" Robbie looked at the picture

and saw a man standing with five children- three girls and two boys. One boy was looking at the camera with the same look he'd come to associate with Nick- angry and determined. The boy had a black eye and a split lip, unlike the others who looked to be in one piece.

It was Jimmy.

CHAPTER 17

Mason stepped out of the home and stood next to a fuming Nick on the cabin's porch. He said nothing, knowing Nick wouldn't hear what he had to say, but offered his silent support. There was silence for several minutes. Mason heard people approaching the cabin when Nick finally took a deep breath.

"He hurt him."

"I saw."

"I'm going to kill him."

"Nick,"

"No, Dad. I'm going to kill him with my bare hands the second I find him. He hurt my *son*." Mason put a hesitant hand on Nick's shoulder.

"I *know* that's what you think the right answer is, son, but it isn't. The other parents deserve to have closure from this, and they won't be able to get it without-"

"None of *their kids* were given a black eye!" Nick looked at Mason and Mason had to fight to not take a step back at the intense *hatred* he saw on Nick's face.

"We'll get him and he'll go to jail-"

"You think that's enough?!"

"No, I don't," Mason replied honestly. "But it isn't for *me* to decide, Nick. Just like it isn't for *you* to decide. We can catch him and present the evidence, but we have to trust the system-"

"That's easy for you to say, Mason. You've always *been* on that side. You've never-" Nick clenched his eyes shut. "If you want justice, you go to a whorehouse. You want to get fucked? Go to a courthouse. It's that simple. And now it's *my son* who will be screwed over."

"What's more important, Nicky? Making sure Jimmy can make it through this, or getting your own justice?"

"You know damn well it's him. It will *always* be him."

"Then let me handle this guy and you focus on Jimmy."

"I can't-"

"Promise me, Nicky. You take care of your son, I'll take care of mine."

"Do you understand what you're asking me to do?"

"I'm asking you to trust me. Not the system, not Russ, not Betty. *Me.* I think after all we've been through this last year, I deserve that, don't I?" Nick looked away.

"He's my *son*, Dad. For the longest time, he was all I had. I'd have killed myself had it not been for him. Everything I have done has been to give him the life I..." Nick turned back to Mason and Mason felt his heart clench at the complete distraught look Nick was giving him. "I promised Carol he would be safe."

"He will be. Once we get him, he will be."

"We got something!" Nick and Mason looked at the FBI agents and Mason narrowed his eyes.

"There's a child." The two left the porch and rushed over.

"It's you!" the young girl cried when she saw Nick. She stumbled to him and fell into his arms, sobbing.

"A-Abby? Abby Hannen?" Nick asked, somewhat recognizing the redhead. With the leaves in her hair and dirt streaked face, he honestly wasn't completely certain, but she nodded. "Can we please get her some water?!" Nick called out. Mason took the bottle from an agent and handed it to the girl.

"You're here too?"

"You know who we are?"

"Jimmy said you would look for us. You're his dad and his grandpa, right?" Mason saw Nick's body tense at the mention of his son.

"We are. Is Jimmy ok?"

"No. King has hurt him. We don't... I think his arm is broken." Nick closed his eyes and Mason struggled not to copy him.

"What about the others?" Mason asked.

"Everyone else is fine. But Jimmy refused to play his game. He said his dad... *you* wouldn't do it, and he wouldn't either," she said, looking at Nick.

"How did you get away?"

"Jimmy caused a distraction for me to run. He said to come back this way and to look for his dad."

"Definitely your son," Mason told Nick in a soft voice. Nick nodded.

"I don't know if I should feel proud, or if I should strangle him." Nick rubbed his eyes. "Wait. You said 'King?' Do you know the guy who abducted you?"

"Yes. He was friends with my mom, or I'd have never… Damien Kingaly. Everyone called him King in school."

"Wasn't he one of the guys you called?" Mason asked Nick, feeling his heart rate increase.

"He was. Said his daughter was visiting his in-laws in Texas. Agent Thomas!" Russ jogged over.

"What do you have for me, Smith?"

"Abby Hannen. Jimmy helped her get away. She said the guy who took them was Damien Kingaly. According to the Fredericks, he was part of their group. He has a child. I didn't think…"

"We'll look into him. Abby, we've got an ambulance on the way, ok? We'll get you checked out-"

"He didn't hurt us. Only…" Abby glanced at Nick. "Only Jimmy."

"Ok. Still, it's procedure. And your mom will be here in just a few minutes. While we're waiting for her, would you be ok talking with my colleague about what happened, and what's been going on since you arrived here?" Abby nodded and Russell led her away to Agent Green.

"Hm. Looks like she has a heart after all,"

Mason said after observing her speaking softly with Abby.

"Did you see which way she came from?" Nick asked.

"Looked like she came from the northwest section there," Mason said, pointing. He saw Nick develop a calculating look. "Don't think about it, Nick. We'll start heading that way in a bit."

"Yeah. I'm going to go find Robbie while we wait for them to get off their asses." Mason nodded and watched him go back into the house.

"Mason!" Betty jogged over. "Did you really find one of the missing kids?"

"We did," Mason said grimly. "Or really, she found us. Abby Hannen. The girl from Louisa. She said they knew the abductor, and that he was only hurting Jimmy." Betty paled.

"How bad?"

"There's a picture of him in the cabin. Black eye, split lip. The bed he was sleeping in has blood on it. Abby said she thinks he has a broken arm."

"Oh no. How... How do you know it was his bed?"

"Because he scratched his name into the wall. Like he was hoping we'd find the cabin and could see he was with them."

"How's Nick?"

"Angry. We'll need to keep an eye on him. He's already said he'll kill the guy if he gets the chance. I can't give him that chance, Betty."

"Then we won't. I'll keep him close by, Mase.

I swear." Betty looked around, frowning. "Where is he?"

"He went into the cabin to find Robbie. Just give me a second." Mason went into the cabin and searched inside. There was no sign of either of his sons. He walked back outside and scanned the agents, looking for them.

There was still no sign. Mason felt his pulse quicken as he looked at the trees.

"I'm sorry, Mr. Johns. My records indicate that your sons were…"

"My sons were what, *Officer Reuben?"*

"They were taken into the woods near your house and… All we could find were bloody pieces of clothing. We believe either the man who killed your wife returned and killed your sons, or they ran themselves and wild animals killed them. Either way, our records show that they're gone." Mason fell to his knees, sobbing into his hands.

No. No, not again. Mason could feel the injured muscles around his heart start to protest- the doctor had warned him about the damage that would always be there because of the sensitive area.

"I can't do this again," he heard himself whisper out loud as he grabbed a tree to steady himself, internally pleading with his body to calm down.

"Can't do what? What's happened, Mason?" Betty asked.

"They're in the woods."

"Ok?"

"The... When I got back from Russia, I was told they were killed in the woods. They're in the woods." Betty looked at Mason. He was sure he looked pale. He had felt the blood drain from his face when he realized they were gone. *Again.*

"Ok. It'll be fine, Mason. We'll find them. They can't have gotten too far, right? Just- just breathe."

"I can't do this again," Mason said, feeling himself beginning to panic. He put the palm of his hand over the scarred area on his chest, pressing down, trying to alleviate the *pain.*

"Then we won't. You're the best at what you do, Mase, remember? You can find them. I'll go with you so we can call it in." Mason nodded. "Ok. Where would they have gone?"

"Northwest."

"Then that's where we'll start." Betty walked over to Russell. Mason knew it was to explain what they were about to do. Russell began gesticulating wildly until Betty said something. Russell looked towards Mason, visibly sighed and nodded. Betty ran back over.

"We get the ok?" Mason asked.

"Yes. Let's go." Mason nodded and took a breath. He could fight through this pain. It was no worse than what had happened to him in Russia- at least there had been less water and electricity... He shook his head. Those weren't memories he cared to relive. He took several breaths before pushing himself off of the tree.

"Are you coming?" he rasped to the girl he considered a daughter.

"Are you going to be ok?"

"Yep," he lied. "But those boys sure as hell won't be once I get through with them." With that, Mason started walking deeper into the woods, worry and *fear* slowly morphing into rage that his sons would be so *stupid*.

CHAPTER 18

Mason and Betty had been looking for what felt like hours, but in reality was only about half an hour.

"I'm going to kill them," Mason growled, irritation showing in his words.

"Nick is just worried, and Robbie was just trying to help his brother, I'm sure."

"I don't care what their excuses are, Wilson! They were given a *clear* order and they completely disregarded it!" Betty winced, glad she wasn't with the men she saw as older brothers.

"They should have known better-"

"Cuffing them to a chair in their hotel rooms," Mason muttered. There was a soft groan and Mason and Betty ran in the direction they'd heard it. Mason stopped short at seeing his two sons face down in the ground together, looking like they'd been knocked out. Mason walked over and looked at them, turning their heads. Nick's head was bleeding from his temple and Mason could see a bruise on Robbie's cheek.

"We need to get them treated," Betty said, dropping to her knees to check over them. "Russ," she spoke into her radio, "we've got them. Looks like someone got the drop on 'em, though. Smith is bleeding and Alderidge has a nasty bruise." Mason gently slapped their faces. Definitely easier than they deserved, in his opinion.

"Wake up, boys!" There was another groan and Mason realized it had come from Robbie.

"Dad?" he asked groggily.

"Yep. Get up, Robbie. We've got to get the EMTs to check you two out and I can't carry you together anymore." He stood up straight and held his hand out for Robbie to take. Once he had, he pulled him up.

"Please no lecture," Robbie begged, rubbing his head.

"Nope. No lecture."

"Thank-"

"Not until your brother is awake and I can yell at you boys together." Robbie groaned and Mason leaned back down to wake Nick up. When he got no response, he put one hand under Nick's knees and one behind his back, hoisting him up.

"Mason, are you *sure* you should be doing this? You know what your doctor said-"

"Who else can?" Mason asked in a strained voice as he took a step forward. *Damn* his son was heavy.

"I can he-"

"You can shut your damn mouth before I forget how old you are, Robert Lucas." Mason saw Robbie swallow. *Good.* Betty walked over to her former professor and gave him a shoulder to lean on as they started walking back to the cabin. The walk was quiet. A very *tense* quiet. Mason started to struggle and shake under the weight of his son. He wasn't going to be able to carry him much longer.

"Dad?" He finally heard. Mason breathed a sigh of relief and stopped. He helped Nick stand on his own feet. "What happened?"

"I don't know. Betty and I found you boys knocked out together in the middle of the woods!" Mason had started off speaking normally, but the relief that both of his sons were ok quickly changed to anger that they were in that position in the first place.

"I had to-"

"Shut your mouth, Nicholas. I don't want to hear anything from either of you until after we get you checked over."

"You can't-" Mason reached forward and grabbed Nick's ear, pulling him close to his face.

"Are you going to shut up, or am I dragging you to the medics like this?"

"I'll shut up." Mason let him go and stormed ahead of them. Nick and Robbie met each other's eyes as Nick rubbed his ear. They slowly followed Mason, also noting that Betty was refusing to look at them. It was another ten minutes before they reached the cabin.

"Mason! You found them?"

"They were knocked out," Mason growled. "My son, the *Green Beret* was *knocked out*."

"What happened?" Russell asked them. The brothers looked at each other and then to Mason, not wanting to anger him any more.

"He asked you *boys* a question."

"He must have heard us calling out to the kids and circled back. He got us from behind," Robbie said quietly. "We didn't see him until it was too late."

"Don't you think there's a reason we go in *teams*?!" Mason yelled.

"We were *in* a team-"

"A P.I. who hasn't seen much action in *fifteen years* and a college professor?! What a team!"

"Mason-"

"No! I am your *father*, Nicholas! You don't get to call me that while I'm chewing the two of you out on how *foolish* your actions were! We had no way to reach you! What if Jimmy had made it back to the cabin?! You would have had no way of knowing! What if one of you had fallen and gotten hurt?! Would you have left your brother to return?!"

"Glad I'm not on that end," Russell muttered to Betty. She nodded her agreement.

"No one was doing anything-!"

"There are procedures the FBI has to follow! They can't go half cocked into the woods! You could have jeopardized this entire case because you were impatient!"

"I'm the only one looking-!"

"Don't you *dare*!" Mason said, shaking in anger. "Don't you dare say that, Nicholas! We are all here for you and for Jimmy! You saw how quick to action this team was when you needed them!"

"I-"

"No! You're *done*! Both of you! Get someone to check you over and then I'm taking you back to the hotel and you *will* remain there, or by God, I will place you under a citizen's arrest for impeding on a federal investigation! Am I understood?!"

"Yes sir," Nick replied with a clenched jaw.

"Clear," Robbie said with a slight blush. The brothers were led away by EMTs and Mason took a moment to breathe. His chest hadn't hurt this badly in months. He needed to sit down... Russell whistled, causing Mason to snap out of his thoughts.

"I've never seen Smith that... submissive." Mason glared at his former partner.

"They're *off* the case, Russ. I warned them when we first started looking that if they separated from us at any point, they were done."

"No arguments from me." Mason turned to Betty.

"That means when they text you for updates, you say *nothing*."

"Got it," Betty said, sadly. Mason rolled his shoulders as he saw Robbie standing and Nick getting a bandage on his forehead.

"I'll be back as soon as I can."

"Take your time. I was trained by the best, so we've got this."

"Damn right you were." Mason stalked over to his sons and crossed his arms. "What's the damage?" he asked the EMTs.

"We can't-"

"I'm their father." The EMTs looked at Nick and Robbie for permission. They both nodded.

"Dr. Alderidge just has a bruise. He'll probably be a bit sore for a while, but he'll be fine. Mr. Smith, on the other hand, should have gone and gotten stitches. He refused with some colorful language and demanded just a bandage."

"We need to get back to the search-"

"The hell you do. You boys are going back to the hotel. As soon as I've got service, I'll be calling your *wives* and informing them of this complete act of stupidity." Nick stood and pointed his finger at his father.

"You're not making me *leave*, Mason. My son-" Mason reached out and grabbed Nick's ear again.

"Want to try that again, *son*?"

"No sir." Instead of letting go, Mason reached out and grabbed Robbie's ear as well.

"Let's go," he growled. He led both of them away from the cabin. Once they were a far enough distance away, he let their ears go. He watched in angered amusement as his adult sons looked at the ground while rubbing their sore ears.

"Please don't make me leave him."

"You were given every chance, Nick. You weren't supposed to have been here to begin with, but the rules were bent for you. Instead of following Russ' lead, you took your brother and went out on your own! If I wasn't taking you to the hotel, I can almost guarantee Russ would have you both in cuffs for interfering in a federal case!"

"My son-"

"When we find him, you'll be given a call just like all the other parents." Mason pushed them to the edge of the forest and unlocked his car when he saw it. "Get in."

"Dad-"

"Nicholas, I am seconds away from getting Russ to arrest you. Get. In." Nick climbed in without another word. Robbie followed his lead, and both were in the backseat again, not wanting to sit with Mason. Mason got in and started the car, refusing to rub his chest. He might be angry with his boys, but they didn't need to see him showing pain. The three were silent as Mason drove to the hotel Lucy and Kaya had found for them to stay, since Nick refused to be out of the same city as his son. When he finally parked, Mason sighed.

"Should we just go back to Leesburg?" Robbie asked.

"That's up to you and Kaya, Robbie. I know Nick won't leave the area. I'm sure he'd appreciate the support."

"Nicky?"

"I'm not leaving. I need to be able to get to him as soon as he's found. If you want to go, go. Not like you're around much, anyways." Mason rolled his eyes and shut off the engine before getting out and slamming the door shut.

"I live in *Florida*, Nick. My entire life is there. Why can't you guys move down instead of giving me crap about moving up?" Nick ignored him and got out of the car. He walked inside, removing his room key as he walked to the elevator. Robbie and Mason joined him as he waited for the doors to open. They all stepped on and Nick pressed the button for the floor where their rooms were located. The bell dinged and they all got off. Nick walked to his room and used his key to open the door.

"-something soon. Nick? What are you- Did you find Jimmy?" Nick shook his head and sat on the bed. "Mason?" Lucy questioned as she and Kaya moved to check over their injured husbands.

"These two boneheads thought it would be smarter for them to separate from the group than listen. The kidnapper apparently saw them and took them out from behind. Betty and I found them knocked out and on the ground. They've been pulled off the case. You will get a call when we find Jimmy." Mason turned to look at his sons. "Don't bother texting or calling anyone. They've been informed to tell you nothing."

"Great. Anything else, Mason?"

"You're to remain in your rooms. They're connected, so there's no reason for either main door to open unless you've ordered room service or pizza." Mason ignored Nick rolling his eyes as he turned his attention to Lucy and Kaya. "If they leave, Russell can have them arrested. It's in their best interest to stay. Unless you and Robbie want to head back to my house."

"We won't go anywhere," Lucy promised.

"We won't either," Kaya told him. Mason nodded.

"I need to head back. Please…"

"We'll keep an eye on them, Mason."

"Ok, then. Nick, Robbie. Please stay here. Seeing you missing once was more than enough. My heart physically can't handle it again." Mason saw Nick's angered look slowly disappear at the reminder of the injury Mason had sustained to keep him safe.

"We'll stay here." Mason hugged his two sons and sighed.

"I'll call you soon," he said before he left. He quickly made his way back to the car and rushed to the meeting point his former team had created, finally feeling the pain begin to subside in his chest. Once he was parked, he hurried back to the cabin.

"Mason! Over here!" Mason saw Russell sitting at an ambulance with a boy about Jimmy's age. He went over to the two and leaned against the opened door.

"You're Jimmy's granddad, right?" Mason nodded. "He said… He said his dad would be looking for us, too."

"He was," Mason promised. "It was getting to be too much for him and he had to step back. Are you Rob Whitten?" The boy nodded. "How did you get here?"

"Jimmy. He caused a distraction and helped Abby get away, and then he did the same for me."

"What about the younger girls?"

"They were still there. He said he couldn't risk it with them. Me and Abby were one thing- we're older. But they're twelve. He said he was going to stay and protect them." Mason nodded.

"That's what I would do, and that's what his dad would do, too."

"I didn't… He kept saying his dad would save him. I didn't believe him. My dad wouldn't-"

"Your dad came to Jimmy's dad begging for help. I went to your house. I promise, everyone was worried about you. Can you tell me about the man who took you?"

"Damien Kingaly. He was a friend of my dad's."

"What about the car he used?"

"It was a green truck. He picked me up after practice. He'd done it a couple times, so I didn't think anything of it. But this time…"

"He drove you to a different city."

"Yeah."

"Did he hurt you?"

"No. Well…"

"Well what, Rob?"

"He made us call him 'Dad.' If we didn't, he wouldn't let us eat. Once we gave in, he treated us like a dad treated his kids. Except Jimmy." Mason tensed.

"What did he do to Jimmy?" he asked in a voice that definitely didn't match what he was feeling.

"Mase-"

"I need to know, Agent Thomas. Nick will want to know once Jimmy's safe."

"Jimmy refused to acknowledge King as his dad, even when I warned him. He said his dad wouldn't give in, so he wouldn't either. I told him his dad would prefer him alive than stubborn, but... King let him eat, anyways. And then he took him into another room."

"What did he do?"

"I don't exactly know. We heard something hitting him and when Jimmy was back in our room, his back was bleeding really bad and he had a split lip. He was crying for his dad." Mason clenched his eyes shut and took a few breaths to calm down.

"Ok. Anything else?"

"After we took a 'family picture,' he told us we were going on a vacation and to change from our nice clothes. He gave us different names, and when he called Jimmy 'Andrew,' Jimmy... He corrected him again. King grabbed his arm and I heard a snap, and then I heard something hitting Jimmy again."

"Mason,"

"I need to just step away for a minute," Mason said, trying to get his stomach under control. He walked to another tree and put his hand on the trunk, taking deep breaths. He was about to return to Rob when he felt his phone buzzing. Frowning, because he didn't think he had cell service in the woods, he brought his phone out and saw it was Lucy calling. He answered it and put it to his ear.

"Mason! Thank God! It's Nick-"

"What about Nick?"

"He went to check on the baby and after a few minutes, I went to see what was keeping him. He's gone, Mason!"

"You've got to be kidding me!" Mason hung up and looked around, anger trumping every other emotion he was feeling as he searched for his son.

CHAPTER 19

Nick heard Mason yelling into the phone and winced. He turned his body and pulled his hat down further, hoping it wouldn't be noticed.

"I don't think you're supposed to be here," Agent Lang said as he heard Mason yelling.

"I got the ok from Jeremy. It's fine. Don't forget *you* are the FBI agent here, Agent Lang. Mason no longer has a badge. You outrank him." Agent Lang gave Nick a smile and nodded.

"You're right. It just feels weird because he's older, but you're right. He's a civilian and I'm an FBI agent."

"Who has agreed to let me search the woods with the group," Nick prompted.

"Yeah, yeah. How'd you even get knocked out? I thought you said you were Special Forces. Aren't you trained for things like that?"

"I wasn't paying attention to what was behind me," Nick admitted. "I got hit on the head with a rock. And my brother has little to no combative skills, so it made sense to take the bigger guy out first." Nick saw the disbelief in the other man's eyes. "My son is missing, Agent Lang. He's my... When it comes to him, all training just flew out my brain and I'm probably about as good as my brother. But no one is going to stop me from at least *trying*. Not even Mason Johns."

"Hm," Agent Lang said, clearly thinking about what Nick had said. Then he shook his head. "You ready to get in there?"

"I don't think so," Nick heard as he felt a hand clamp down on his shoulder. "Nicholas Mason Johns, you have five seconds to start heading back to the car." Nick cringed as he turned to face his father.

"Dad..."

"Get the hell out of here, Nick. I won't say it again." Nick straightened his back and looked into Mason's eyes.

"You don't have jurisdiction here-"

"I do as your *father*!"

"And if I was under eighteen, that would hold up. If I had been *raised* by you, I'd likely stay away out of respect, and I'd trust you to bring Jimmy home to me. But I'm forty, and I was raised in foster care. I grew up thanks to the Army. You being around now is because I wanted to get to know you, and because I wanted Jimmy to have a relationship with you. You don't have a *legal* reason to keep me away, and I don't... respect you enough as my father to blindly obey. So no, Mason. I'm here and I'm going to find my son."

"I'll keep him safe, sir," Agent Lang promised.

"I'll stay with a group this time," Nick offered. "But I need to find him. You said you gave up on us, and to not be like you. This is me following your advice, Dad." Mason looked around and saw a search party forming behind him and Agent Lang.

"No matter what I say?"

"No matter what you say. Jimmy isn't going to feel like I abandoned him."

"I need you to stay safe, Nicky. You might be Jimmy's father, but I am *yours*. I can't lose you again."

"You won't." Mason put a hand on Nick's face and rubbed his thumb on Nick's cheek.

"Then I'll see you in a bit."

"Thank you." Mason nodded and dropped his hand.

"I love you, Nicky."

"I know, Dad." Mason stepped away and Nick squared his shoulders.

"Wow," Agent Lang whistled.

"What?"

"Nothing. Just wish my dad was that open about how he felt about me, you know?"

"Are we going to start looking, or what?" Nick asked, uncomfortable with discussing fathers and feelings with a complete stranger.

Agent Lang began to move deeper into the woods. Nick kept a sharp eye out and listened as best he could with people calling out for the missing girls and Jimmy.

Why were they calling for *his* son? He didn't even know the people looking- Nick stopped thinking about it and breathed. These people were taking time out of their day to search for children they didn't know, simply because they were missing. He should be grateful.

The search continued for hours. Nick was tired and hungry.

But he'd been tired and hungry before. That was nothing new. He refused to stop looking for his son. Jimmy needed him more than he needed a break.

"Jimmy!" Nick frowned and turned. Sure enough, Mason was there, calling for Jimmy. They met eyes and Mason nodded to him. Nick turned back around and trudged forward.

"We've got to call it a night," he heard. Nick saw a local deputy talking to Agent Lang. "It's getting dark, and we can't put these people in danger for some kids who might not even be-" Nick clenched his jaw and closed his eyes as he turned his head. He felt a hand on his back.

"He's right- about it getting dark, at least," Mason told him softly. "We need to get you back to Lucy." Nick shook his head.

"No."

"Nicky,"

"No, Dad. I've done searches in dense areas like this in the dark before. If I can do it for strangers, I can do it for my son."

"Oh, so *now* you can fall back on your training?"

"That's not fair," Nick said, glaring at Mason.

"It wasn't meant to be. You've already been

knocked out once today, Nick. Where was your training then?"

"I had a minute of distraction. You can't-" Nick sighed and reached in his pocket, pulling out a light that wrapped around his head. He looked at Mason and handed him a second one.

"Son,"

"You said to trust you. This is me trusting you. At least this way, you'll be able to make me stay alert." Mason took the light and put it on his head.

"I have a condition, then."

"I don't have any more-" Mason grabbed some rope from his own pocket and pulled it through a single belt loop on his pants before tying it into a knot. He held the other end up to Nick.

"I'm not losing you in the woods again."

"How- why- how long have you *had* that?"

"I grabbed it the moment you said you were going to join the search party. I had a feeling, and I wasn't going to let you wander around at night on your own with no way to contact me."

"I still have no way-"

"Russ agreed to stay at the cabin and Betty gave me her radio." Nick sighed and held his hand out for the end of the rope, quickly tying it to his own belt loop.

"I feel like I'm on a leash," he muttered.

"You *are*. Betty knows we're going. Let's go before we're forced to head in." Nick nodded and the two continued their trek deeper into the woods. Nick winced at every crunch of the leaves under his shoes. He kept switching from looking at where he was stepping and straight ahead to where he was going. At sunset, Nick switched on his light. Mason held off on using his, relying on the light still available and the light Nick was giving off. It wasn't much longer before he turned his light on as well.

"What happens when we find him?" Nick asked quietly, stepping over a fallen tree. Mason pulled out a rectangular device from his pocket and held it up for Nick to see before returning it to safety.

"Betty slipped me a GPS."

"She thinks of everything," Nick said, shaking his head in slight amusement.

"She had a decent teacher. And it's not her son or grandson who's the subject of the search. You're scattered, Nicky. Not that I blame you."

"Unless it causes me to get knocked out," Nick muttered.

"Because you broke protocol, boy." Nick grew quiet again as they listened for any sound out of the ordinary. Other than the sounds of their footsteps, the cicadas, and an occasional owl, it was silent.

"Sh," Nick said after another hour of them searching alone. "Did you hear that?" Mason held his breath, listening.

"Voices."

"We need to get closer."

"Carefully," Mason agreed. "It could just be some campers, kid."

"Doesn't hurt to look." Mason nodded and allowed Nick to lead them closer to the sounds. The voices were getting clearer, as well as the sound of a fire popping.

"Young girls," Mason noted.

"Adult male," Nick added. They crept closer and saw the light of the fire.

"Damn it, Andrew! You have slowed us down too many times today! We have people trying to take you three from me, and we have to keep moving! We don't have *time* for your stunts!" Nick frowned, clearly disappointed.

"My name isn't Andrew!" Jimmy. Nick heard the unmistakable sound of skin striking skin and then a thud with the teenager crying out. Nick moved to step forward, but felt the rope holding him back.

"Mason, that is my *son*! Now let me go or I swear I'm cutting the damn-" Nick stopped when he realized Mason was speaking quietly into the radio.

"That's right, Thomas. We have a visual on Jimmy and the twin girls, as well as who I'd assume is Damien Kingaly. Yeah. Look, I can't guarantee-" There was another cry and Nick looked at Mason with tears in his eyes.

"Dad, please-"

"*Green, Wilson, and I are close, Mason. Just hold on.*"

"You said you were staying at the cabin," Mason spoke into the radio.

"*If you two can walk in the dark, we can too. Just give us five minutes, Mase. Please.*" Mason looked at Nick, who had a look of sheer desperation on his face.

"No promises." Mason allowed Nick to step closer and they saw Jimmy on the ground in a small clearing. The light from the fire showed tear tracks on Jimmy's face and Nick tried to move closer- only to find himself pushed to the ground.

"Let me up!" he whispered harshly.

"Not until you get yourself under control," Mason told him as he kept the weight of his chest on his son.

"He's *hurting-*"

"I know, Nicky. It's killing me, too. But we need the extra manpower, ok? Jimmy will understand. Please son. Just a few more minutes."

"Mason," they heard a voice whisper.

"Down here." A light beamed on them and Nick knew he heard Agent Green chuckling.

"Let me up, Mason." Mason got off of Nick and helped him up.

"I'm sorry-"

"Save it. Can we *please* get him now? Or are we going to have dinner first?"

"Stuff it, Smith," Agent Green whispered.

"Wilson, you and Green go around the left. Mason and I will go around the right."

"I didn't carry-" Russell reached under his

pants leg and handed a second weapon to Mason.

"And me?" Nick asked.

"I'm not arming a guy who I can't prove knows how to shoot under pressure."

"I was a Green Beret," Nick argued.

"You are too involved, Smith!" Russell hissed.

"And Mason isn't?"

"Mason was trained how to deal with intense situations like this by *our* standards. I saw how you were with Anderson. You're not getting a gun." Russ and Mason walked almost silently away and the female FBI agents seemed to glide to the opposite side of the men. Nick watched the two pairs inch closer, the teens and their captor none the wiser.

"Damien Kingaly, FBI. Drop the knife and step away from the children!" Nick felt his heart beat wildly at Betty's announcement that this madman had a *knife* near his *child*. He crouched down and started walking slowly towards the missing children.

"I'm on a camping trip with my children! I've done nothing wrong!" Kingaly proclaimed.

"We're not your kids!" One of the twins cried. Kingaly moved to backhand her and Nick struck. He leapt from his position in the trees to the clearing, knocking Kingaly down. Kingaly sliced at Nick with the knife, but Nick grabbed his wrist and slammed it on the ground over and over until the knife fell out. Betty darted to the two and grabbed the knife, sticking it in an evidence bag she had on her.

"Well?" Nick asked, looking up at Russell and Agent Green. "Are you gonna cuff him?" Russell grabbed his handcuffs and stalked over, glaring at Nick.

"Are you *ever* going to let me do my damn job, Smith?"

"Not when my *son* is on the line," Nick said angrily. He waited until Russell had his hands on Kingaly before he jumped up and rushed to Jimmy, who was still on the ground.

"Be careful, Nicky. You shouldn't move him. We don't know what sort of damage has been done." Nick ran a gentle hand through Jimmy's hair before resting his forehead on Jimmy's. His son was unconscious, there was no argument there. But he was *alive*. Nick would take it. For now.

"He shouldn't have internal injuries-"

"*Shouldn't*, but it's not a guarantee. We need to wait for paramedics to assess him before we move him," Agent Green interrupted. Nick glared at her before turning to Mason.

"Do you have a pocket knife?"

"I do. Why?"

"Can I borrow it?" Mason shot a glance towards Kingaly, who was sitting against a tree by Russell, handcuffed. "I'm not going to attack him, Mason." Mason took a breath before sticking his hand in his pants pocket and pulling out his pocket knife. He held it out to Nick.

"I want it back, Nicky. This was my father's," he said as Nick wrapped his fingers around it. Nick nodded and flipped out the knife. He put the blade under Jimmy's thin shirt, sharp side up, and sliced the material until he could tear it himself. Nick handed the pocket knife back to Mason and grabbed Jimmy's shirt, tearing it up to his son's sternum.

"Can someone shine a flashlight on him?" Nick asked, having somehow lost his headlamp in the struggle with Kingaly. Betty held her light over Nick's shoulder and Nick, more gently than she'd ever seen him work, touched over Jimmy's abdomen.

"What are you doing?"

"Internal bleeding usually has some sort of swelling. I'm not feeling anything out of the ordinary, so I'm going to move him instead of waiting for paramedics."

"Smith, you *can't-*" Russell tried to advise.

"I'm his father, and I'm giving myself permission!" He took off his jacket and draped it over Jimmy's exposed chest before he picked him up, doing his best not to jostle him.

"You got him?" Mason asked softly.

"I got him," Nick answered. He looked at Jimmy's face and leaned down to whisper. "I'm here now, Jim. Daddy's got you."

CHAPTER 20

"Are you going to be able to carry him the whole way, or should we-?"

"I can carry my own son," Nick heard himself snap to Mason.

"I didn't mean it like that, Nick," Mason said in an attempt to placate him. "But you haven't eaten anything today. You've barely had any water-"

"I've gone through worse for less. My kid needs me and I'm going to be the one who holds him."

"Mr. Smith?"

"Yes?" Nick responded to one of the weather-named twins.

"Is Jimmy going to be ok?"

"After some time, yes."

"Good. He was really brave." Nick tightened his grip on his son.

"He is. He always has been."

"Did Abby and Rob make it to you?"

"They did," Mason told the girls.

"Ok. Did they tell you how Jimmy hurt his arm worse to make sure they got away?"

"Not... exactly. They just told us he caused a couple distractions."

"We tried to help. King got mad at us, too,

but Jimmy made him even more mad to keep us safe. He kept telling King how you would save him and us."

"Jimmy knew nothing would stop me from finding him."

"I should have killed the brat when I had the chance." Nick stopped and turned, shining his headlamp into Damien Kingaly's eyes.

"Do you have any idea who you threatened?"

"A brat who-" Kingaly grunted and bent forward.

"I am so sorry about that," Russ said from beside him. "My flashlight slipped from my hand. I've actually considered taking it in to be checked because sometimes I think it truly has a mind of its own." Nick smirked and turned back around, continuing the long walk back to the cabin and the ambulances that would be waiting for them.

"Are there bears?"

"Hm?"

"Bears. King said there were and if we ran off, they'd eat us."

"Bears are more scared of you than you are of them. They'll make themselves look big, but if you just yell at them, they'll run. Unless they're mother bears with their cubs, but we should be ok. If they see our lights and hear us talking, we'll be ok."

"Are you ok, Mr. Smith? Jimmy doesn't seem to be very light."

"I've carried him before. I'm fine, but thank

you for checking. Are you two excited to see your parents and brother?" Nick asked the twins.

"Yeah," one of the girls answered.

"Yes. I hope Marty treats us like Jimmy did. He told us he was going to be a big brother soon. He's going to be great at that."

"I had no doubt," Nick said with a small smile. "But I appreciate you girls talking him up. That'll make him feel good."

"Is it ok if we send him letters and call him?"

"You'll have to ask him when he's awake," Nick said as he carefully shifted his son. "I doubt it'll be a problem, though." He heard Mason chuckling behind him and had to fight his own laugh at the girls' hero crush on his son.

"Still doing ok, Nicky?"

"I've carried a two-hundred something pound man across a desert to safety with people shooting at us. I've got this."

"Is that when you got your award?"

"Hm? Oh, that. That story isn't... Jimmy doesn't even know it, and I'd like to keep it that way. Keep his innocence a bit longer." Nick quietly sighed, realizing a lot of his son's innocence had been stripped this weekend. The things he'd tried protecting him from...

"I see the lights," Betty announced from beside the twins. "Not much further."

"Am I allowed to ride with him to the hospital?"

"It should be an agent-" Agent Green started

to say.

"But if he's unconscious, then it'll be fine. We'll meet you guys at the hospital. And Smith, you should get your head checked out," Russell told him.

"Yeah, ha ha."

"No, I'm serious. The bandage is soaked with blood."

"Look at me," Mason demanded. Nick turned his head and Mason narrowed his eyes. "You're taking care of your son and then you're getting stitches. Don't bother arguing, Nick."

"We'll see. If he wakes up, I'm not going to let him be alone longer than he needs to be." Nick refused to concentrate on anything else but the flashing lights of the ambulances. As soon as he got close enough, there was a stretcher waiting for him for Jimmy. Nick carefully put him down, feeling like someone was squeezing his heart at Jimmy's moan.

"How long has he been unconscious?"

"About forty minutes. From the reports of the other kids, he likely has a broken arm-" Nick looked down and swallowed at the obvious bulge of his son's arm. "Definitely has a broken arm," he corrected. "Lacerations likely across his back-"

"We'll take care of it," an EMT said. "Has someone contacted the kids' parents?"

"We have," Betty said. "The parents of the twins are meeting us at the hospital, and Mr. Smith is this young man's father." The EMT looked at

Nick with a sympathetic glance.

"I can only carry one extra person with me."

"It'll be his dad," Russell said, flashing his badge. "He won't let anything happen to him, and we'll meet them at the hospital." The EMT nodded and they carefully loaded Jimmy into the ambulance with Nick climbing in behind him.

"I'll meet you there, Nicky," Mason promised.

"Please get Lucy."

"I will," Mason said before the doors shut. Nick turned his attention to Jimmy and tried to stay calm after seeing him in better lighting.

"Poor kid," he heard.

"His back," Nick told them. "From the other boy taken... I think he was whipped. But please- his left arm is broken." The EMT nodded and she and her partner carefully rolled Jimmy onto his side. Nick could see the strips of blood on his shirt and felt nauseous. The two EMTs finished cutting his shirt and slipped it off of Jimmy, revealing the crisscrossed stripes with bruises all over the teen's back.

"Dear God," Nick whispered, suddenly feeling faint at seeing what had happened to his son.

"Dad, you good there?" Nick blinked away the black spots from his eyesight.

"Just lightheaded. I'll be fine." One EMT put an immobilizer on Jimmy's arm as the other checked over Nick.

"Have you had anything to eat or drink today?"

"There have been more important things to concern myself with." He was handed a cold bottle of water.

"Drink this, and then I want to have a look at your head."

"I was told I needed stitches, but-"

"More important things, huh?"

"That's my son on the table. He was taken because parents asked me to find their kids. I... His mom died when he was three. I promised them both I'd keep him safe. Drinking and eating doesn't seem as important as keeping my promise."

"But now he really needs you and you're-"

"I'll eat as soon as I hear he'll be ok. I've been longer without. A few more hours won't kill me." The EMTs left it alone as they continued to the closest hospital.

"We're getting close. You won't be able to stay with him very long, Dad."

"Not leaving him until I have to." The ambulance arrived and Jimmy was unloaded. Nick kept up the pace with him as nurses wheeled him through the doors.

"You have to wait here, sir. Someone will come and get you when we have answers." Nick watched with wet eyes as his son was taken from him. He stood still for a while, and then began to pace.

"Nick!" Lucy ran into his arms and Nick

buried his face into her neck.

"He looks so bad," he whispered. "His arm is definitely broken and his back…" Nick stifled a sob as he recalled the bloody lines and bruises on Jimmy's back.

"He'll be ok," Lucy told him, clinging to him.

"Is there any word?" Nick looked up and saw Mason and Robbie standing with Russell and Betty.

"Not yet."

"Ok. I'm sure it won't be long." Nick leaned against the wall, holding Lucy's hand.

"How are you feeling? I feel like I've completely ignored you…"

"I'm feeling fine, Nick. Nauseous and scattered, but fine. And I don't feel ignored. I feel like the wife of a dedicated father. I can think of worse things." Lucy put her free hand on her lower abdomen and sighed.

"I'm afraid," Nick told her quietly.

"I am, too." Their hands grew tighter together.

"James Smith's family?" Nick stood up straight at the doctor's voice.

"We're his parents." The doctor walked towards him and Lucy.

"James has a fractured arm. He'll be in a cast for at least six weeks, and I'll send whatever records needed to your doctor for James to be accurately cared for. He has a broken rib as well, and it was close to lacerating his liver. We had to perform emergency surgery, which is why you hadn't heard anything until now. The cuts on his back were not too deep, but they'll take some time to heal, especially with the care he'll need for his rib. Unfortunately, they'll likely scar..."

"Can we see him?"

"He's in the Pediatric ICU and he hasn't woken up from his surgery yet. You're able to go up to the third floor and wait for someone to get you, but it will have to be one at a time until he's moved to a regular room."

"When will that happen?"

"When he's ready," the doctor said with a shrug. "It'll be a day or two."

"Will I be able to stay with him?"

"No, I'm sorry," the doctor told Nick. "I'll allow everyone to see him, even though visiting hours are over, because I was informed of what happened to him, but that's all I can do tonight. You can be here at seven in the morning at the earliest, Mr. Smith."

"I can't leave him-"

"Nick," Mason warned, seeing the doctor becoming frustrated.

"I'm sorry, Mr. Smith, but this is hospital policy. If you make an issue with it, then I can't see you being allowed back at all. I'd hate to do that with the circumstances surrounding your son, but I will if I have to." Nick bit the side of his cheek, but he nodded.

"We appreciate you letting us see him," Lucy told the doctor.

"This was... We're just glad the children are safe." The doctor walked away and Nick hugged Lucy to him.

"He said third floor, right?" Robbie asked.

"Yeah. Nicky? You ready to go up and see him?" Nick nodded to Mason and he and Lucy led the way to the elevator.

"We'll just come back in the morning," Betty told the group. She and Russell went the opposite direction from the family.

"You should get your head looked at," Lucy quietly told Nick.

"After I see him." The group took the elevator to the third floor and then moved to the waiting room.

"Are you here for James?" a nurse asked after seeing the group.

"We are," Mason answered. "Parents, grandfather, and uncle."

"Ok. He's waking up. I can take you back one at a time, but then you'll have to go." Lucy gently pushed Nick towards the nurse.

"Go, Nick. Go see he's ok." Nick nodded and followed the nurse down the hall, turned a few times, and then she motioned to the door.

"He's right in there, Mr. Smith." Nick nodded and opened the door a bit. He heard steady beeping and saw Jimmy in the bed, pale and seemingly lifeless. The paleness caused his bruised face to stand out worse than when Nick saw him in the ambulance. Nick heard a sob come from his throat and he backed out of the room, falling to his knees.

CHAPTER 21

Nick watched the steady rise and fall of his son's chest through the wires. His baby... He hadn't seen him like this since he was a newborn, when they'd almost lost him. Carol had had an emergency C-section and Jimmy and his brother- Nick closed his eyes. Jimmy was *fine*. The doctor had said the most recent X-rays showed the surgery took. His liver was safe for now, but they still wanted to keep him another night or two- just to be sure. Ribs were tricky.

"Dad?" Jimmy muttered. Nick blinked back tears. Jimmy had been calling for him and Carol in his sleep. The doctor told him it was the morphine causing the request for his deceased mother. Nick stood and adjusted the blanket over Jimmy's small body. He leaned down and kissed his forehead.

"I love you," he whispered. With one last look, Nick left Jimmy's room. He made his way to the parking lot and took a breath before putting on his helmet and starting his motorcycle. He drove to the nearby gym and parked before he pulled out his duffle bag from the side bag and walked to the door. Nick scanned his membership card and watched the light blink to open the door. He walked in and immediately went to the locker room to change into a pair of shorts and a tank top, storing his bag in a locker. He knew what he was there for and sat on the bench, wrapping his hands.

Nick walked to the gym and saw the punching bag was free.

Good.

He went over to it and put his headphones in his ears, blasting his music. He raised his fists and positioned his body, and then landed the first punch. Another punch. A third. A kick- and then the bag became Damien Kingaly.

Nick snarled at it, unaware of the frightening sound he had made that caused people to step away from him. The bag bore the brunt of the pain he wished he could give to the man who had hurt his child. The pain he wished someone would inflict on *him* for allowing this to happen to Jimmy in the first place. He punched until he felt his lungs were about to cave in. He stopped and leaned against the wall, trying not to sob. What had he allowed his job to *do* to his child? He felt a finger tapping him and he pulled out his headphones.

"You done?" A tiny girl asked him. "Other people would like to use the bag, too, you know."

"My apologies," Nick sneered. He followed gym etiquette and wiped the bag down. He watched as the girl attempted to do what he had done as he went to throw the towel away and had to force back a laugh.

"That's *rude*, you know. Didn't your parents

teach you manners?"

"My mom was murdered and my dad was a POW in Russia. When would they have taught me?" Nick responded, crossing his muscular arms.

"Well boohoo. Everyone has a sob story. You still should have learned not to *laugh* at people-"

"Then you should learn how to properly use a punching bag."

"This is what you were-"

"*Look* at me. Doesn't it look like I *know* how to use it? These were standard in my training-"

"For what? Assassins-R-Us?" she muttered.

"Close enough," he smirked. "Don't- You're going to hurt yourself if you keep trying to do what I did without any training."

"Then train me, oh wise one." Nick rolled his eyes and turned off his music before stepping over to her. He held the other side of the bag.

"First, take off the gloves."

"I'll hurt myself."

"You need to get the *stance* right first before you add power. It might feel good at first, but it'll be harder to control the swing of the bag. I watched a buddy of mine nearly break his nose with how crazy his bag went." The girl dropped the gloves.

"Now what?"

"Hold your arms like this," he said, showing her how to have her fists near her chin. "Back straight, feet apart, and make sure you're steady."

"Like this?" Nick went around the bag and

physically adjusted the girl.

"Like *this*. Take it slow at first. You're about to use muscles you didn't know you had."

"I'll say. I didn't know they could bulge like that in real life." Nick said nothing as he went to the other side of the bag.

"Punch. One fist at a time. Slowly until you get a feel for it." He watched as the girl followed his instructions.

"When can I add the kicking?"

"Focus on the punching."

"SMITH!" Nick rolled his eyes and looked beside him at Agent Thomas.

"What?"

"When'd you become a gym trainer?"

"When people are about to hurt themselves trying to do what I can do. What do you want, Russ?"

"How's Jimmy?"

"Who's Jimmy?" the girl asked, looking between the two. "Are you *gay*? Damn it!" Nick smirked.

"Not gay, but happily married. You weren't going to get anything, kid."

"I'm twenty, thank you."

"And you're about five years older than my *son*. Ask the trainers if you have any other questions." He grabbed his phone and headphones and motioned for Russell to follow him to the locker room.

"Jimmy?" Russell asked again.

"Mending," Nick said before taking a sip of water. He saw himself in the mirror and grimaced at how soaked with sweat he was. "Doctor thinks he might be able to go home in two days."

"That's good…"

"What are you doing here?"

"Mason said you'd be here blowing off steam."

"Yeah, well… You wouldn't let me have five minutes with Kingaly. What else am I supposed to do? How did you even get *in*?"

"I flashed my badge at the door. Someone opened it for me. At least *some* of the people here have manners. And I'm here because the charges were officially issued. Five counts of kidnapping, child endangerment, assault of a minor, and… they added attempted involuntary manslaughter with the rib."

"Hm. He attacked me and Robbie, too, you know."

"And you weren't following orders when he did that. I can add those charges, but you two will face penalties if I do because then it'll go on record." Nick frowned at the man and crossed his arms.

"What's he looking at without the assault?"

"If it sticks, he's looking at a lengthy sentence."

"*If?*"

"The kidnapping and assault will stick for sure. That's a near guarantee sentence of ten years, possibly fifteen depending on how he'll plead." Nick sat on the bench and started unwrapping his hands.

"And with the assault?"

"Maybe another year for the two of you combined." Nick nodded.

"Leave it out. I took the brunt of it, and this could ruin Robbie's career."

"That's what Mason thought you'd say."

"And this required an in-person visit to me instead of a phone call to my father?"

"He thought you might like to hear it for yourself."

"Oh, yeah. I love hearing how this bastard's going to get away with hurting my kid. Fifteen years, Russ? Have you *seen* my son? Have you heard him crying out for his mother- the one who has been dead for over ten *years*?"

"Have you?"

"I'm there as often as I can be," Nick growled.

"When he's asleep."

"What do you want me to say?!" Nick yelled as he stood, towering over the man. "I *failed* him, Thomas. My *son!*"

"And that means you can't be there while he's awake?" Nick ignored him as he threw open his locker and changed his shirt, opting to shower at home.

"Move," he demanded when Russell blocked him from leaving.

"The rest of your family might be too afraid

to tell you this, *Smith*, but I'm sure as hell not. Get off your ass and be with your son. He was traumatized by a madman. You remember what that's like? To be traumatized? To want your parents, only to have nothing and no one to comfort you? Because I'm damn sure that's how your son is feeling right now."

"You have no right-"

"Maybe I don't, but the people who *do* have the right don't know how to tell you that you're just making this worse! It's killing Mason, Smith, and whether you want me in your life or not, he's important to me so you're stuck with me- and Betty, too. You didn't see-" Russell stopped and shook his head.

"Great. You have a better relationship with my father than I do. Anything else you want to rub salt on, Thomas?"

"You have a family, Nick. Things like this can either pull a family apart, or bring them even closer. I've seen families pulled apart too many times. Please don't hurt my friend."

"Is that all?"

"No."

"Then what else could you possibly have to say, Russell?!"

"You stink. Get a shower before you see your kid." Nick narrowed his eyes as the agent walked out of the locker room.

"Jackass," he muttered.

CHAPTER 22

"Hey, kid." Jimmy looked up and smiled as Mason walked into his room.

"Hi Grandpa. Are you here to take me home?"

"Not yet, Jimmy," Mason said with a sad smile. "Doctors want you here for a few more days. Your rib-"

"Yeah, yeah," Jimmy said as he carefully leaned back in his bed.

"They just want to make sure there's no more chance of it screwing your liver up. Once it's just a bit better, you're going home. I promise."

"Is Dad going to visit today?" Mason's smile tightened.

"Hope so."

"Hm. I've been here for almost a week, Grandpa. He hasn't visited once."

"Yes he has-"

"Not when I'm awake." Jimmy's shoulders slouched. "I just want to see my dad."

"I'll let him know, kid. How've you been? Still having nightmares?"

"Not so much now. Russ came to see me yesterday with Betty. Told me Damien Kingaly is being charged with as much as they can stick him with."

"Yeah. They told us that, too."

"Has Dad…" Jimmy sighed. "Did he look for me?"

"Kid, I had to threaten to tie him to a chair to get him to slow down with his search for you. He stopped listening to Russ and the other agents. He and Robbie went off on their own to look for you!"

"Really?"

"Really. And he was the one who got the team to your location. It was dark and he'd come prepared with headlamps for the two of us. Don't tell him I told you, but I made him tie a rope to his belt loop to make sure he didn't get too far from me," Mason said with a wink. "But your dad was the one who carried you from where Kingaly had you three to the ambulance. He was in the ambulance with you and waited here for hours, Jimmy."

"Where is he now?"

"Hey." Jimmy and Mason looked at the door and saw Nick awkwardly standing there. Jimmy noticed the damp hair and frowned. "Can I…?" Jimmy nodded and Nick stepped in the room.

"I'll just go get us some lunch," Mason offered. He walked out of the room and Nick went closer to Jimmy, sitting on the bed near Jimmy's legs.

"Hi," Nick said again. "I'm, uh… I'm sorry you haven't seen much of me-"

"What was more important than me?"

"Nothing. I've been here every day, Jim. And

I know it's been while you were asleep, but... I just didn't think you'd want to see me. I haven't been the best company lately. But I stopped at the house to shower before coming here, and the detective outfit for the bear finally arrived. I thought you might like to help me get it together so we could give it to Lucy. And since I was home, I grabbed your charger and... a few other things." Nick moved his arm and showed the bag he was carrying. He reached inside and brought out the Army bear from Jimmy's room.

"Why?"

"Because I didn't want you to be here alone. I'm sorry, Jim. It was stupid-" Jimmy reached out an arm for the bear and Nick handed it to him with a small smile.

"Thanks."

"How are you feeling?" Jimmy shrugged and made a face, putting his cast-less hand over his injured ribs.

"It hurts, but I'll live. You went through worse, right?" Jimmy panted.

"This isn't about me, son. I went through worse because I chose to," he said, even though Jimmy knew he'd had a rough childhood in foster care. "I had the option to quit at any time. It was out of sheer stubbornness that I stayed. But you..." Nick looked away and took a breath.

"When I'm back to normal, will you teach me how to fight and protect myself?"

"What?"

"I don't want this to happen again. If I can fight, it won't, right?" Jimmy looked at Nick and saw a flash of anger go across his face.

"No."

"But-"

"This won't happen again, Jimmy. No one will ever use you to stop me again. There's no need for you to have to fight."

"You can't promise something like that, Dad."

"I can, Jim. I'm... I've thought about it, and I'm quitting my job as a P.I. I'm going to get a normal nine to five job. You can continue to be homeschooled if you'd like, or we can enroll you in public school. But I've got to do this to keep you safe. You and the baby."

"Dad-"

"My mind is made up, kid."

"But you love your job." Nick put a hand on Jimmy's face.

"But I love you more. Let me keep you safe, Jimmy." Jimmy looked away and he heard Nick sigh. "I'll be back tomorrow. You've got your bear. And here's your phone charger, so you can reach me at any time, ok?"

"'K."

"You'll be home soon, Jim. We can talk about school once you're more comfortable." Nick ran a hand through Jimmy's hair and walked out of the room.

Jimmy felt the tears welling up in his eyes.

It was his fault his dad was quitting.

It was his fault his dad didn't think he could protect himself.

CHAPTER 23

"Welcome home, Jim," Nick smiled. Jimmy walked through the front door and sighed. The couch was made up for him to sleep on so he wouldn't have to be stuck in his room. Nick urged him forward and led him to the couch.

"Thanks."

"Not a problem. Can I get you anything?"

"No." Nick's smile faltered for a second.

"Ok. Well, I'll be at the table if you need something. Here's the remote. Just yell if you need me."

"Where's Lucy?"

"She's packing things up at the office."

"Should she be doing that?"

"She's not lifting anything heavy. She just wants to help and be supportive." Nick ruffled Jimmy's hair and went into the dining room. His laptop was still set up and he picked up where he'd left off with the job search.

It wasn't long before Lucy walked into the house. She greeted Jimmy with a gentle hug before going to Nick. She leaned against his back and wrapped her arms around Nick's neck.

"How's it going?"

"Ok, I guess. Not a lot of jobs hiring people with my skills."

"So don't quit," he heard Jimmy grumble. Nick sighed and closed his laptop with one hand as he used the other to rub his eyes.

"Jim, I can't have something like what happened to you happen again. I just can't."

"Then teach me how to protect myself!" Nick turned his head and looked at his son. The bruising was faded, but still evident, and his arm was still in a dark blue cast.

"No," he simply told Jimmy. "This won't happen again, so there's no point."

"Damn it, Dad-"

"Jimmy, I am trying really hard to be patient with you, but talk to me like that again, and you'll be grounded for a week. Do you really want to be grounded while recovering?"

"No."

"Then quit it. And I don't want to hear another word about learning how to fight again, do you understand me?"

"Yes."

"Thank you. Now why don't you go hop in the shower?"

"Is that an order?"

"No, Jimmy. It's just a suggestion." Jimmy pushed himself off the couch and went down the hall.

"He just wants to learn how to protect himself, Nick. What's wrong with that?" Nick slammed his hand down on the table and jumped up.

"He doesn't feel safe with me!"

"What?"

"He doesn't trust me to protect him, Lucy," Nick told her with tears in his eyes. "And who can blame him? He was with me when Kingaly took him! So now he wants to protect himself because he doesn't think I'll be there for him." Nick fell back into a seat and hid his face in his hands.

"Nick..."

"Don't Lucy," Nick sniffed and wiped at his face. "I'm doing this to keep him and the baby safe. I won't let this happen again. If that means giving up doing what I love and what I'm good at, then so be it. I'll find something else. Something safer." Nick opened the laptop back up and continued with his job search, ignoring Lucy trying to get him to talk about changing his mind.

CHAPTER 24

Jimmy gently sat on the couch, careful not to aggravate his aching ribs worse. He rolled his eyes at the drink and pills Nick had obviously set out but took them nonetheless.

"Hey. How was your shower?"

"Warmer than Dad," Jimmy told his stepmother with a lopsided shrug. Lucy sighed and sat on the couch beside him.

"He's scared, Jimmy."

"Yeah right. He's ashamed of me, Lucy."

"What makes you say that?"

"Because I failed. Look at me! My face, my rib, my arm, my back... This never would have happened to *the* Nick Smith. He's ashamed that I'm his son because he wouldn't have turned out like this. He would have protected the others and took Kingaly down because that's him. And now he feels obligated to stay with me because he doesn't think I'm worth teaching."

"Oh, Jimmy," Lucy said sadly. "That's not how it is at all."

"Then why, Lucy? I just want to be like my dad, but he doesn't..." Jimmy sniffed and wiped at his face, wincing as the cast scratched his cheek.

"You should talk to him-"

"So he can threaten to ground me again?

Yeah right."

"I doubt he'll-"

"It's fine, Lucy. I'll just... I'll see if Uncle Robbie will take me in for a while."

"Jimmy."

"Dad doesn't even want me here. I'm causing him to stop doing what he loves because I'm just not good enough. It'll be best for everyone if I'm out of the picture. Let him focus on the new baby. Maybe this one won't be as much of a disappointment." Lucy blinked back tears and left the room. Jimmy didn't see her pulling out her phone.

Twenty minutes later, there was a knock at the door before Mason just walked in, dragging Nick by the collar behind him.

"I told you, Mason, I was prepping for an interview!"

"And I told you, your son needs you!" Mason pushed Nick to the couch and pointed a finger at him. "Now you will sit here and you will talk!" Mason walked to the front door and stood, blocking Nick from being able to leave. Nick sighed and leaned against the back of the couch.

"I'm not teaching you to fight," Nick started.

"Ok."

"Ok. So are we done?"

"I want to go live with Uncle Robbie." Nick turned and looked at Jimmy with wide eyes.

"What the hell did you just say?"

"I want to go live with Uncle Robbie," Jimmy

repeated. "I'm obviously a burden to you and Lucy-"

"Don't you dare call yourself a burden, James Robert. You could never be a burden to me."

"Then why can't I learn how to protect myself?"

"Why do you want to learn?!"

"Because I don't want you giving up your life for me. I'm sorry I wasn't good enough-"

"You stop right there. Where is this coming from, Jimmy?" Jimmy swallowed and wiped at his face with his cast-less arm.

"Because I couldn't protect myself and the others. I let you down."

"Jimmy..."

"Because if I could have protected myself, he wouldn't have hurt me. You wouldn't be ashamed of me, and you would have visited me in the hospital," Jimmy said, ending in a whisper. Nick stood up and paced in front of the couch.

"Dad, I need a minute alone with him, if you wouldn't mind." Mason nodded and stepped outside. Nick stopped in front of Jimmy and put his hands on his waist. "I was there every day, Jim. But I couldn't see you awake in the hospital."

"I know-"

"Do you know why? Do you know the truth about why I couldn't see you?"

"Because you were ashamed-"

"Yeah. Yeah, I absolutely was ashamed." Jimmy blinked and the tears fell down his cheeks.

"I was ashamed of myself, Jimmy. I should have protected you. When I saw you that first night in the hospital... It was my fault you were there. It was my fault you were taken because if it weren't for my job, you would have been safe. Do you know what you being taken did to me, Jimmy?"

"You found me-"

"After hours of crying into my father's shoulder, going into shock, and sleeping in your bed," Nick admitted. "I could barely function, son. You don't realize how important you are to me, do you?"

"But you won't-"

"Because I can't teach you! Do you not trust me to protect you? Am I not good enough?"

"You are-"

"Then why are you pushing me away?!"

"Because I don't want you to be ashamed of me!" Nick narrowed his eyes and crouched in front of Jimmy, taking his good hand into his.

"Because of you, we found you and the Fredericks twins. Abby and Rob were safe. You put your life on the line to keep it that way, and while I want to strangle you for being so careless with your own life... I have never been more proud, Jimmy. You went above and beyond... I don't think I could have been as brave as you were. That whole time, he was hurting you and all you could think of was keeping the others safe. I would have been focused on keeping myself safe- especially at your age."

"Really?"

"I was an absolute mess, Jimmy. If it wasn't for Mason… I wouldn't have snapped out of my shock. I would have been useless to you. But you? You were strong, son. So much stronger than me."

"You're not ashamed of me?"

"Absolutely not. And I'm sorry that my pride made you think that, Jimmy. I thought… I thought you didn't trust me to protect you because this was my fault to begin with."

"I don't blame you," Jimmy said, frowning. "I just… I tried doing what I thought you would do." Nick snorted.

"You must see me as a hero, then, Jim. And that's one thing I'm not. I'm a stubborn jackass who doesn't like to be told no. Someone comes to me and hands me a case, and I get excited to see who I can piss off next. No. *You* are the hero, Jimmy. And I've been having to beat off reporters nearly every day because they want to interview the teenager who sacrificed himself to keep other kids safe."

"How would they know?"

"Because the families you helped want you to be honored for keeping their kids alive and getting them back to them."

"He wasn't going to hurt them as long as they played his game," Jimmy shrugged.

"That might be true, but he looked ready to snap when I saw him. You pulled his attention off the girls and onto yourself." Jimmy pulled his hand away from Nick.

"But I don't understand why you're quitting being a detective. You love it."

"My being a P.I. put you in this mess. I couldn't bear…" Nick looked away and Jimmy saw Nick's nose turn red. "You and this baby are my entire world, Jim. I'm ashamed I let something I enjoy put you in danger. I'm ashamed I couldn't protect you. So if that means I find another job to make sure you stay safe? It's not even a question of if I'll do it, Jimmy. You are more important to me than my job."

"But you love it."

"I love you. I enjoy being a P.I. but I love you."

"What if I want you to keep being a P.I.?"

"Sometimes the parent knows what's best, kid. In this case, me getting a new job is what's best."

"I don't like it."

"You don't have to." Nick stood and ran a hand through Jimmy's hair. "Are… are we ok, now, Jim?"

"You're not ashamed of me?"

"Not one bit."

"Then we're ok."

CHAPTER 25

Eight weeks later

Nick drove the car to his office. He was finishing getting the furniture moved out, but the lease was set for another four months. The rent was expensive, but it would be worse to break the contract. He parked in what had been his parking spot for over a decade and cut the engine.

"Are you *sure* about this, Dad?" Nick gave Jimmy a small smile.

"I'm sure about keeping you two safe. Now you said you would help, or was that a lie to get you to come with me and try to talk me out of this again?" Jimmy shrugged with a smirk.

"Being stubborn is hereditary." Nick chuckled and got out of the car.

"I'm still going to put you to work." Jimmy lifted his arm.

"Doctor said to take it easy or I'd be right back in the cast."

"And I'm not planning on you doing a lot of heavy lifting right now. Mason will be here soon enough to help with that." Jimmy and Nick went into the office and Jimmy looked around.

"It looks weird."

"It does," Nick agreed. He took a look around the office as well. The place where he and Jimmy were able to bond after his wife died. The place he met Lucy, where they fell in love. The place- Nick swallowed. "Can't get sentimental, kid. Go clean out the fridge for me, will you?"

"That's *disgusting*. I'll clean out my area and *you* get the fridge." Nick smirked.

"I can do that. Remember, if anyone comes in-"

"You're not accepting new clients or cases. I *know*, Dad."

"I don't think I *ever* had an attitude like you do when I was your age."

"You have it *now*," Jimmy told him. "Where else do you think I got it?"

"Brat."

"You need to clean the fridge." Nick ruffled Jimmy's hair and grabbed a trash bag from the box on Lucy's desk before going back to the kitchen. Jimmy shook his head and went to fix his hair as he started cleaning the section of the office he'd used since he was five years old. He had gotten a few things separated when he heard the doorknob jiggling. Thinking it was his grandfather, Jimmy kept his back towards the door, continuing with his sorting.

"Excuse me. I'm looking for Sergeant Nicholas Smith?" Jimmy tensed and turned. He saw a man who, except for the dirty blonde hair, could have been his father's clone. Muscles, height, even the tattoo.

"Uh... Dad?"

"Yeah, kid?" Nick came to him, wiping his hands on a dish towel. "You ok?"

"There's someone looking for you."

"I told you-"

"He said 'Sergeant Smith.'" Nick's smile dropped and he turned to the door. He saw the man and tensed.

"What the hell do you want?" he spat.

"I need your help-"

"And when I needed you after my wife-?"

"I'm sorry, Nick. I was grieving, too." Jimmy's head tilted.

"You knew my mom?" The man turned to Jimmy.

"I didn't... Jimmy?"

"Yes?" The man looked at Nick.

"He doesn't even know who I am?" he asked.

"I don't see how that's my fault," Nick said, crossing his arms.

"Can someone explain how I'm supposed to know this guy?" Jimmy demanded.

"Staff Sergeant James Douglas," he said, sticking his hand out. Jimmy shook it.

"Nice to meet you, I guess. How did you know my mom?"

"She was my baby sister." Jimmy pulled his hand away and looked at Nick.

"I have another uncle?"

"No."

"But he said-"

"It's complicated, Jimmy. I need you to go

into my office for a minute and wait for Mason."

"But-"

"*Now*, James." Jimmy went into Nick's office and shut the door. In a form of teenage defiance, he pulled the blinds up on the door and stood there, watching. Nick shook his head.

"He's gotten big-"

"It's been ten and a half years since you last saw him," Nick reminded James.

"I know-"

"And now you're here asking for a favor? Give me one reason, James. *One.*"

"I'm your brother-"

"No. No, you're not. I *thought* you were. I saved your life. You introduced me to Carol. I named my *son* after you. But after she died? I needed my brother. I needed you, James, and you told me-"

"I know what I said, Nick. I've never been more ashamed of myself, and now I've missed out on my nephew's life-"

"What the hell are you doing here?"

"I heard you were a detective."

"No."

"You're... here..."

"I'm cleaning my office out. I have a new job that starts next week. I'm not taking any cases, and I'm sure as hell not taking one from you."

"Please, Nick." The door opened and Nick saw Mason walking into the office.

"Hey," Mason said with a small frown after

looking at James. "Everything ok in here? Where's Jimmy?"

"My office. And everything is fine. He was just leaving," Nick informed his father.

"Nick, please- I *need* you. I introduced you to Carol and that got you Jimmy. Surely that's worth some favor, right?"

"The favor was not decking you the second I saw you in my office. Now you need to leave or I'm calling the police."

"Frank's been murdered." Nick froze.

"What?"

"Frank has been murdered. Execution by a Beretta M9. He was the only one I kept in contact with from our unit after... her accident. I..."

"You what, James?"

"I'm being set up for his murder."

"There's no way-"

"A contact I have... My DNA was found at the scene. This was my last stop before they arrest me."

"And what exactly do you want me to do about that?"

"Prove it wasn't me."

"Maybe I shouldn't. Maybe I should let them just arrest you and charge you. At least then I'll know you won't drop in like this on me again."

"Then Frank's murderer will get away with it. Don't let your hatred of me get in the way of finding the truth for him."

"I'm not a P.I. anymore. I can't help you."

"Nick-"

"But I have some... friends in the FBI. I'm sure they'll-"

"No. No Feds." Nick ignored hearing Mason's snort.

"Why not?" Nick asked, rolling his eyes.

"Because..."

"I need an answer, James."

"The last person Frank talked to was a Fed."

"Ok?"

"Agent G... I can't remember, but there was definitely a 'g' in the name." Nick frowned.

"That doesn't help at *all*."

"I *know*. But Frank cancelled on me for lunch to meet with the Fed and we rescheduled for drinks later. Next thing I know, he's *gone* and I'm being called saying my DNA has been found at the scene with a gun Special Forces is known to use. I hadn't seen him in two weeks, which was why we were getting together. You've got to believe me, Nick."

"Nicky, maybe we should-" Mason tried to say before he was interrupted.

"How about you back off, old man? This is a family conversation." Mason raised his eye.

"How about *you* back off?" Nick scowled. "He's more family than you are. That's my *dad*."

"I thought he was dead?"

"He's obviously not. Look, James, I... If I wasn't about to start a new job, I'd help. Frank was a good guy and a good friend. But I've got my own family to think of, too. I've got Jimmy, and my wife is-"

"You remarried? I thought Carol was it for you."

"Why does it matter? The entire family cast us aside once she died. Why should I talk to you about my current wife? Why should I reach out? Jimmy's own *grandmother* sent me back pictures of him *shredded*. No, James. Find… Find someone else." Nick turned away and went back into the kitchen. Jimmy saw him leave and hurried out of the office.

"Is he going to help?" Jimmy asked.

"I don't think so. He was my last chance." James turned and limped towards the door.

"Why are you limping? Sorry. That was rude." He turned back to Jimmy and gave him a small smile as he pulled up his pants leg, showing a prosthetic leg.

"Lost it in Afghanistan. Your dad saved my life. He carried me from where the bas- bad guys were shooting to our base, shooting at them and dodging them shooting at us. Got a nifty award for it and everything."

"*That's* why he got that award?" Mason wondered aloud.

"Yeah. I introduced him to my sister after that…"

"Carol," Mason said.

"Carol," James confirmed. "My baby sister. But it's… It's alright. After her accident… Nick's right. We couldn't accept he was here and she wasn't and we cut contact with him. Now that I need him, well, I don't blame him for not wanting to help me. *I* wouldn't help me."

"We can do it," Jimmy said, looking at Mason. "Right Grandpa?"

"Absolutely not, Jimmy. Nick would kill me and I doubt you'd taste freedom for quite some time- and knowing your dad, I'd bet you'd also lose the ability to sit for a while. No. He said he can't help, so we won't."

"But he's family. What if it was Uncle Robbie who needed him and he was treating him like this?"

"Jimmy,"

"*Please*, Grandpa? Just because Dad's given up being a P.I. doesn't mean we have to give it up with him."

"I can't do that to him, Jim. I won't." Mason patted Jimmy's shoulder and walked back towards the kitchen to see Nick.

"I know what you're going to say," Nick said as he scrubbed the fridge.

"Oh?"

"He was the closest thing to a brother I had before Robbie came back. He's my son's uncle, and he needs help. But I *can't*, Dad. If I agree to his case, then it'll just be harder and harder to say no."

"We all know how much you love this job, Nicky. Jimmy still feels like it's his fault you're quitting."

"It *isn't*-"

"I *know*. I know. But maybe…"

"What?"

"Maybe this is the sign you need that it's not time to quit yet. Jimmy's fourteen. He's bounced back from what Kingaly did. He's eager to help his uncle, and I know *you* can solve your friend's murder and keep Carol's brother out of jail. And just think of what he'll owe you now?"

"I want eyes on Jimmy at *all times*. And Lucy, too."

"I think that can be arranged. Does this mean-?"

"Just for this case, Dad. I owe it to Frank, and I owe it to Carol to be better than her family."

Nick and Mason left the kitchen to let James know they'd take the case. When they got to the main room, James and Jimmy were nowhere to be seen.

"You've got to be kidding me!" Nick frantically searched his office and then opened the door. James and Jimmy were standing at a car, talking. Nick ran forward and pulled Jimmy to him, hugging him tightly.

"Dad? Ow!" Jimmy rubbed his smarting behind. "What did I do?"

"You were *just* kidnapped, James Robert! You didn't think I would panic at not seeing you in the office?!"

"I'm sorry. I was just telling Uncle James goodbye…" Nick looked up and glared at James.

"You don't remove him from my office again, do you hear me?! You lost that right-!"

"Nick. He couldn't have known about Jimmy." Nick just hugged Jimmy to him tighter. "As for you, Mr..."

"Douglas," James supplied.

"Mr. Douglas. Nick and I will take your case. It won't be pro-bono, however. I'll have his assistant write up an invoice. Our fees are a $200 non-refundable down payment before we get started, and then depending on the case, it's $100-$300 per hour."

"Seriously, Nick?" James asked.

"I'd have charged you a flat out fee of fifty grand. You want my services, James? You don't get the friends and family discount anymore. Agree or be on your way."

"Alright. I agree to hire the... Blue Hat Detective Agency if it means you'll keep me out of jail."

"It'll be a pleasure doing business with you, Staff Sergeant Douglas." Nick turned to Jimmy. "Now you let Mason take you home while I get some more information. I'll text Lucy and let her know you're grounded for the rest today and tomorrow."

"Aw, *Dad*!"

"Don't, Jimmy. Dad, you mind?" Mason motioned for Jimmy to follow him. Nick waited for the two to be in the car and driving off before he turned his attention to his former brother-in-law.

"So."

"So," James repeated. "Where do we start?"

"I can't believe I'm doing this. I have a feeling this is going to be the worst mistake of my life."

EPILOGUE

Nick winced as the metal bit into his wrists. The arresting officer seemed… *gleeful* to make the cuffs as tight as he could. Nick knew he shouldn't have baited the man, but it was just in his nature to not know when to stop.

"Turn." Nick clenched his jaw and turned to the left of the camera for his… mugshot. How had it even *gotten* to this?

That's right.

James Douglas, the bastard.

"Turn." Nick turned to the right. Lucy was going to kill him.

The pictures were done, fingerprints taken, and Nick was led to a holding cell.

"You get one phone call," the officer told him. "I'd make it count if I were you." Nick was taken to a phone near the holding cell and given some *slight* privacy. He sighed as he took the phone off the hook and dialed a number he was suddenly glad he'd memorized.

"*Wilson.*"

"Betty, thank God. I need your help."

"*Nick?*"

"Yeah. I'm in Fort Meade… in jail."

"*What are you doing in jail?*"

"Took one last client before permanently

retiring and the bastard didn't tell me he was NSA! So going into his house tripped some sort of alarm- I need you to get the office key from Lucy or Mason and get me *proof* that I had permission to be there and then bring it to Maryland. Can you do that for me?"

"Nick... You know I would, but-" Nick felt his stomach drop.

"But what?"

"I'm on my leave. I'm with my family in Louisiana."

"Shit."

"I'll call Mason-"

"No! No, he told me not to go without him."

"The only other option I have is Russ." Nick saw the officer tap his watch.

"Alright. Yeah, just not my dad, ok? He'll kill me." Nick frowned as he heard Betty laugh.

"I'll hang up and let Russ know to get the paperwork from your desk. What's the file name?"

"It's under Staff Sergeant Asshole."

"You're not serious."

"Well if your brother-in-law blamed you for your wife's death by a drunk driver and then cut you and your son out of his life, what would you call him?"

"I'll get Russ there as soon as I can. Why didn't you just call the guy?"

"Because he's on house arrest at my former mother-in-law's house, and if he's an asshole, she's a bitch. I'd rather have admitted being in jail to my dad. Look, the cop's giving me the stink eye. I've got to go. *Please* beg Russ not to tell Mason. I don't think I could stand hearing that lecture." The phone cut off and Nick sighed as he put it back on the hook.

"Still scared of your daddy, hm?"

"Former FBI. Wouldn't you be?" The officer smirked and led Nick back to the cell.

"Enjoy, Mr. *Smith*. Who knows how long you'll be here." Nick sat on the bed and rested his head in his hands.

He knew he should have just punched the bastard when he walked into his office.

Lucy was going to kill him. Mason was going to skin him alive. And Jimmy... Hopefully Jimmy wouldn't *ever* find himself in this same predicament.

"Hurry up, Russ," he groaned into his hands.

ABOUT THE AUTHOR

Meagan Diehl

Meagan Diehl was born in Hampton Roads, Virginia. She has a degree in English and spends her time reading, writing, and watching crime TV shows and just about anything Disney.  Meagan also has a love of history, especially Virginia history and Greek mythology, and Marvel Comics. She continues to reside in Hampton Roads with her husband, three children, and their two dogs.

BOOKS IN THIS SERIES

The Blue Hat Detective Agency

The Yellow Ribbon Murders

Nick Smith was five years old when he saw a man brutally murder his mother. He spent thirteen years in foster care, waiting for a father who had seemingly vanished overseas while on deployment with the United States Army. After serving his country himself, Nick became a private investigator to give him the resources he needed to solve the death of his mother. After years of building his reputation as an investigator in Leesburg, Virginia and struggling as a single father, Nick takes on a last minute client who will change his world forever. SSA Mason Johns has spent nearly twenty years searching for a serial killer who goes after the wives of deployed soldiers. When he gets a call about the killer's newest victim after a decade of silence, Mason and his team leave for Leesburg, Virginia to confirm the killer's return, only to come into contact with the town's local private investigator.Mason begrudgingly agrees to work with the arrogant Nick Smith to find the man who has ruined countless lives. In doing so, it reopens a past Mason thought he'd left behind.

A Family Affair

After successfully capturing the serial killer responsible for the death of his mother, Nick Smith has found his career is now in the spotlight. But when a new client reaches out to Nick for help, it sets him on a path he never dreamed he would have to walk. With former FBI agent Mason Johns at his side, Nick embarks on his most difficult case yet- a case that hits closer to home than anything he has ever worked on previously. A case that could very well end his time as a private investigator.